FORGETFUL WATERS

MARIE SIBBONS

PROLOGUE

The brightness of the sky is wondrous tonight. Every star in the universe must be making an appearance, radiating a myriad of dying glows through the darkness of space and time. It is said the stars visible on Earth no longer exist and are merely the remnants of a life long gone. Just like a person in a photograph. But she doesn't want to believe something so beautiful is not really there.

Even the moon appears so much closer than usual. She reaches out to touch the vast golden ball in the hope she will be energised by its cosmic rays. But of course, it is an optical illusion. The moon isn't really golden. Rather, it is a lump of dull rock many thousands of miles away, a giant version of the one she is sitting on, the one that is now digging into her legs.

What is she doing up here alone? That's right. She's meeting someone. But she can't remember who it is. The inside of her head feels like the sea below, tossing and filled with froth. What was she drinking back there?

An unseasonal brisk breeze sweeps across the headland causing a moment of soberness and she trains her ears to listen out for footsteps between the lapping of the waves.

There is something. Someone. She can hear shuffling ... yes, footsteps. The steps are getting louder, and she wonders if she should be afraid. Seagulls are cawing loudly, and for a moment, she loses track of the other sound. There it is again, stronger this time.

Ahead of her, the outline of a person begins to emerge, and her heart misses a beat. It disappears into the sea mist, and she thinks she may have imagined it. Then it reappears and steadily grows larger as it comes towards her. It is him. He is here and is smiling at her, his eyes glistening in the near darkness. She cries out with relief, running towards him before suddenly stopping. She can see something else glistening like the stars so far above them. As the steel slices her arm, she cries out in pain. The blade rises up again and she steps back to avoid it, falling into the dark water below.

CHAPTER ONE

How long has she been in the water? It could be days or just hours because all sense of time has vanished. Her arms and legs are rigid and numb, and an icy hand grips her frozen throat. Only her stinging ears can experience the pain of being pummelled by the relentless waves. And, of course, her lungs which are begging for air. But there is no air. There is only water, so much water. If only she knew how she got here, she could contemplate swimming to safety. Perhaps she should still try because life is worth fighting for. And there is so much of her life left to live. Fight! Keep going! But which way? There is only blue darkness around her. Apart from the moon and the stars. Her chest is on fire, a final warning. She opens her mouth, a final gasp for life. Nausea saturates her dying body. Now she is beneath the water, twisting around with no grasp of direction. It is ending at last.

***

She opens her eyes. The violent punching inside her head is paralysing, and she can't swallow without a searing pain sending shock waves through her brain. Beneath her, the rigid mattress tortures her tender back, so she knows it isn't her own bed. Nor is it her bedroom. Where is she? The sparsely furnished room is uncomfortably bright and the air around her is a mixture of staleness and disinfectant. A rhythmical beeping comes from somewhere close by, along with the irregular pattern of footsteps pacing tiny distances. One step forward; two steps back. Closing her eyes once again, she begins the mental task of figuring out why she is lying in a hospital bed.

There was a party, she is sure of it, but she can't remember whose. In fact, she is struggling to remember the identity of anyone at all ... even her own. Who is she? It is such a simple question yet the thick blanket of fog filling her mind is a formidable obstacle to the answer. Perhaps if she starts with the letter A. Anna or Belinda or Catherine? No, no and no. Donna? No. Emma? Yes, that's right. She's Emma. But the relief that sweeps over her at this first victory ends abruptly because there are more challenges to face.

Why is she, Emma, in hospital? Where was she immediately before she was brought here? The fog returns, but this time it is thinner. Not bothering with the alphabet, she juggles with the most likely scenarios – was the party in a club or someone's house? Her parents' house. Yes, that would be it. Probably. Something awful obviously happened there, an accident which resulted in her lying in this unyielding bed.

There is a shadow to the right of the bed but her neck is too stiff to turn, so the hazy shape remains only in her peripheral vision. She senses it is a person even though the dark form is silent and motionless. If only they would speak. If only she could speak. It is no good as so much concentration seems to intensify the punches in her head. She wishes she could go back to sleep and wake up in a few hours feeling less awful. That's what she usually does when she feels this rotten - buries her head under the quilt and sleeps off the pain. But she isn't in her own bed. And she's never felt this rotten.

Seconds turn into minutes and more of her senses creep back into life. Her tangled hair smells like seaweed and feels like it, too. Salt cakes her shrivelled tongue. Burning reflux tortures her throat. There is only one explanation for the state of her body; she was swimming in the sea and got into difficulty. And something is telling her that her parents live by the sea therefore that must have been where the party was. So, another question answered. Maybe.

If she was with them, they must have been celebrating as a family. But what? If only she could remember. Whatever the occasion, she obviously drank way too much. That would explain her mashed-up head. And parties have cocktails. Yes, cocktails make her black out. Yet, she doesn't feel sick. And she always feels sick after drinking too much, especially when cocktails are involved. At least, she thinks she does.

At last, several blurred words and the outline of a picture is forming. Things are starting to come back to her now. There's a man, a boyfriend. His name floats inside her head, but she can't grab hold of it. After a few minutes, she is able to see his distorted features. He hates her drinking because he thinks it uncouth. It's strange how this is the first thing she remembers about him - his criticisms and disapproval of aspects of her lifestyle. He can't be much fun.

But she wishes he was with her now. That shadow cannot be his or he would be holding her hand, kissing her face, saying how much he loves her. So, where is he? Perhaps he doesn't love her anymore. Maybe they argued. Yes, she has a feeling they quarrelled. But he would never hit her, she knows that. Perhaps they were walking by the coast, and she tripped in the darkness, banged her head on a rock then fell into the sea. And her head is hurting like mad.

Despite the pain, she closes her eyes again and concentrates harder searching her battered brain for fragments of the immediate past.

She is in a manicured garden. On a grey flagstone patio, a glossy white table, adorned with empty glasses and a jug of orange juice, reflects the sun into her eyes. Two square-shaped presents, perfectly wrapped in silver paper, sit in the centre. The azure sky is as vibrant as the shade of the perfectly cut lawn. It is a fanciful picture, as artificial as an image on a jigsaw puzzle lid. But the idyllic scene is not just visual. Piano notes are filtering through an open Georgian window. Her father is playing the instrument so melodically. She recognises the tune though cannot remember the name. It is on the tip of her tongue. There's Rosa, serene as ever. She is dancing by herself on the luxurious green grass, her slender arms curled like a ballerina. No, she is waving wasps away from the orange juice, but they keep coming back. Finally, she covers the glassware with ivory napkins and removes one of the presents. Emma wonders why Rosa isn't talking to her even though they are standing close together, just feet apart. She calls out to her friend, but Rosa does not respond. Maybe they argued, too. Yes, they've argued a lot lately and this causes her heart to ache with sadness. At last, Rosa turns and meets her gaze.

'How are you feeling?'

'Like hell,' Emma replies, though she knows the words are still in her head.

'Your pulse rate is high? Are you in pain?'

'How do you know that? You can't feel my wrist.'

Rosa's strawberry blonde hair and pale skin morph into the dark features of a tall gangly man. Instead of a pastel blue sundress, he is wearing a pinstriped suit with a tie clipped back at the breast pocket. He does not resemble a midsummer garden party guest.

'Can you hear me, Emma? My name is Dr Syed, and you are under my care.'

Disoriented, it takes a few seconds to relocate her mind. Of course, he is a doctor because she is in hospital and not in her parents' garden. Now things will become clear. A cluster of half-formed questions balance on the tip of her tongue. Forcing the other ones back, she attempts to ask the most important. *What happened to me?* But although the words leave her brain, they are too weak to carry forward into sound.

'Can you let me know if you are in pain? Nod your head or lift your hand if you cannot speak.' His clipped accent sharpens the compassionate words.

She gives a painful nod even though he is no longer looking at her.

'I shall have the nurse bring you something to ease your discomfort,' he says, still not looking at her. Then he is gone.

Dr Syed's consultation is as effective as it is brief. Knowing he is taking care of her, calmness seeps through Emma's body like a tumbling comfort blanket even though her head still throbs like it is mixing concrete. She doesn't know which is worse – the thumping or the fog.

Within minutes, a young man wearing an odd boilersuit appears. Balancing a tablet in one palm while gripping a thimble of water in his other hand, he says, 'This will make you sleepy.'

She wonders why a porter is handing out medicine to patients but doesn't care enough to ask. She grabs the water and swigs back the tablet. Remembering her manners, she forces her lips to rise at the corners before her eyelids come down like a protective curtain. Almost immediately the pain eases allowing the fogginess to take hold.

Once again, she is in the garden, but the vibrant colours have altered. Now there is white everywhere, so many dull white drapes like those covering furniture in abandoned stately homes. Drapes in the garden? The image sharpens. No, they are giant tents, not drapes. Oh yes, marquees. A marquee means a grand party, but where are the guests? Apart from her, the garden is empty. Rosa must have gone inside probably wanting to escape the wasps. She hates wasps. But there is no sign of them either. No sign of any life. Even the music has stopped. Then her parents appear, and warm relief sweeps over her. It is as if she hasn't seen them for years even though they meet most days. She imitates Rosa by waving her arms in the air, but they make no response. Her parents don't see her. Instead, they take the orange juice and glasses inside leaving only the single present on the otherwise bare table. Her mother doesn't like wasps either, so it was a daft idea to put fruit juice outside on a summer evening. The sun hides behind a cloud and her skin prickles. She wants to follow the others into the house, but her legs are fixed to the ground. Then a shadow stretches across the grass until darkness envelops her.

'Are you feeling better now?'

Flickers of white cut through the darkness and she is back in the hospital room watching the fluorescent light above her. 'Yes, thank you.' She wonders if she's been asleep although it only seems like seconds, minutes at the most, since she shut her eyes. If she has slept, it couldn't have been for long. The man has sat down in the chair next to the bed and is reading her chart, an action she considers impertinent. Whatever is wrong with her is none of his business. But when he scribbles on the chart, curiosity takes hold. 'Who are you? What are you writing?'

'Just updating your meds. Nothing more.'

That kind of makes sense, she decides. He's given her pain killers so needs to write it down, even if he is a porter. 'Why are you dressed like that?'

The man smiles. 'My name is Staff Nurse Mason, but just call me Paul.'

Oh yes, she thinks. Of course, male nurses can't wear dresses so the overall must be their special uniform. Her interest in the hospital worker vanishes as quickly as it appeared. 'That's nice, Paul. Is ...?' She can't think of the name or even the person she wants to ask about. It isn't Rosa and that's the only name she has. 'Are my parents here?'

The nurse raises his eyebrows before shaking his head. 'Not that I'm aware of.'

'They may have been here already. There was someone sitting here earlier,' she says, pointing to her right.

He smiles. 'I doubt it, but I can double-check for you.'

'No, please don't bother. I won't be here much longer.'

'It's no bother. Do they live locally?'

Emma starts to answer before realising she doesn't know where she is. 'Which hospital are we in?'

'Stanford General,' he replies.

Emma thinks for a minute. 'Did it used to be called something else?'

'Did what used to be called something else?'

'This hospital.' What else?

'I don't think so. It was only built about twenty years ago.'

'Twenty years. I don't recall that name. Where are we?'

'Stanford.'

She gives up, not liking the sarcastic tone coming from the strangely dressed nurse who is probably wrong anyway. She will find out soon enough herself when that man arrives, the one whose name she can't think of. Or maybe he's been here already. Maybe he was dozing himself so didn't notice that she woke up for a while. She turns her head to the right. Nothing. There is only a bare wall without a chair or a visitor. Not even a shadow. She must have imagined it. They must have had a serious argument for him not to visit her. Yet neither have her parents. It is strange that they haven't been in touch, especially if she was at their house when the accident happened. What was the accident?

The realisation hits her – he might be hurt, as well. What is his name now? Her mum and dad, too. Her mind spins so fast that she cannot focus enough to breathe. She turns to ask the nurse if he will ring them after all, but the chair is empty. Did he know what was on her mind? Has he gone to fetch someone more senior to break some horrible news to her? She recalls his expression when she first mentioned her parents.

Something is wrong because they wouldn't leave her, their own daughter, alone in a strange hospital. Her heart pounds as fear overwhelms her. Please don't let them be dead, she whispers to the air around her. Bile rises in her throat as she splutters and cries out for help. But nobody comes. Shouting gives way to sobbing, and she drops her tired arms over her face as if they could hide her from any horror coming her way.

Footsteps are in the distance, a mixture of clomping and clicking but, unlike earlier, moving in the same direction. They are gaining momentum, gradually getting louder. Uneven but regular, the footsteps clearly belong to more than one person, and they are coming her way. She attempts to count the number of different treads. One, two. Please let it be my parents, she thinks. She prays, too.

The grey metal door opens and two people enter the room. The first is a youngish woman wearing a similar uniform to the male nurse. She is followed by a man, older and more distinguished looking, and his face is etched with concern. Is he bringing her bad news? Of course, he is. Her body begins to tremble.

'You've got a visitor,' the nurse says.

The distinguished man stands unmoving for a few seconds and Emma watches with dread as the creases in his face deepen. What is he going to tell her? Why doesn't he just get it over with?

He remains rigid with one hand on his cheek as if deep in thought, unaware of the apprehension filling the room. Then he rushes over to the hospital bed and takes Emma's cold wet hands in his. 'My darling, I've been so worried about you. Thank goodness the doctors say you're going to be okay.'

Emma screams.

CHAPTER TWO

Her father's face appears in the blackness of her mind. His sandy hair is neatly cut, and, unusually, he is wearing a black tee shirt. He looks younger than she remembers him being. Or is it just that he is happier today? Her mother teases him that he always looks more handsome when he smiles. It is rare to see him displaying emotion, let alone joy as his moods and thoughts are so often a closed book. Not now. But his face is at an angle, and she knows he isn't smiling at her. It must be at her mother even though there is no sign of her. Behind him is a huge red balloon in the shape of a heart. It begins to float upwards, but he grabs the attached string and pulls it back to him. He stands proud holding the string like a standard bearer in battle. The balloon has swayed to the side in the breeze and bobs above his head. Two silver digits are now visible against the cherry red. Twenty-five. Her father is standing closer to her. She reaches out to touch his face, but his image fades away to nothing. The balloon drifts into the distance.

***

'I don't know who you are. I've never seen you before in my life. No. Don't come near me.' Emma is barely able to breathe between the screams and choking arising from her mouth.

The bemused nurse watches on as the male visitor grabs Emma by the elbows.

'What? Calm down, Emma, it's me, David. Thank God you're all right,' he says. 'When I heard it was you in the water, I thought I'd lost you. Let me hold you.' The more she struggles against him, the more forcefully he holds her.

'No. Let me go. Take your hands off me ... please.' With each panicked phrase the decibels increase, and she finally gets her wish. He steps back from her, his face as white as the bedsheet she is gripping in terror. 'Nurse, get him out of here.'

'Mrs Sims, please,' the nurse shouts. 'You cannot behave in this way. Mr Sims has driven hours to get here. He wants to take you home, but the doctor will need to agree first.'

Emma stares at the nurse having only heard the first part of the sentence. 'What? Home? He's not here to take me home. Don't listen to anything he tells you. I'm not going anywhere with him.'

The nurse lets out a sigh as she glances at her watch. 'Try not to upset yourself, Mrs Sims. Your husband has been very worried about you.'

'Husband! What are you talking about? He's a total stranger. Get him away from me.'

'Now come along, Mrs Sims,' the nurse says.

The man steps forward once more. 'Darling, we were at the boathouse. Don't you remember?'

'Get him away from me.' Emma keeps her eyes fixed on the nurse. 'I want my mum and dad. Where are they? Why aren't they here?'

Emma glares at the man now standing slightly back from the nurse, his mouth open wide, his pallid complexion gradually turning purple. While he continues to meet Emma's gaping eyes, the nurse touches his arm and whispers something in his ear. Words connected to concussion and confusion pass between them. He nods. She cracks a joke. Emma watches them convinced it is all an act. She considers the possible reasons behind the crazy situation coming up with only two – kidnapping and removal of a murder witness. Either the nurse must be involved in the deception, or he's bribed her. What about Dr Syed? Doesn't he already earn enough money to make him immune from corruption?

The nurse and man identifying as her husband continue their conflab while Emma observes them with a mixture of suspicion and terror as they whisper, wave arms, and shake heads. In contrast to her own incoherent rantings, the man sounds well-spoken and articulate. The persuasive type. She needs to get away before he convinces the already exasperated nurse to give them some privacy. A frantic scan of the small room gives her little hope of getting past her captors, but there is a window next to the bed.

Her hands shake violently as she pulls the blanket away before sliding her weak legs over the side of the bed. One foot touches the cold tile floor, the first step towards her escape. As she pushes forward putting her weight on both feet, the whisperings cease. In less than a second, she is lying prostrate on the floor tiles her feeble legs having collapsed under the strain of supporting her whole body. Her strength has left her, and willpower is not enough. Unable to sit up she clenches her fists and bangs her head repeatedly crying out in frustration at her helplessness. She feels a hand grabbing her wrist and screams louder until realising it belongs to the nurse. 'She's still in shock, Mr Sims,' she says, taking Emma's pulse. 'Perhaps you should come back tomorrow when she's had time to come around properly. I'll get the doctor to check over her before he leaves the ward.'

Mr Sims shakes his head before removing his glasses and rubbing his face. His skin has turned white once again. 'I appreciate she's in shock, but did you hear what she said before? She thinks her parents are – '

'Please, Mr Sims.'

'But she's so confused,' the man continues, his voice less measured than earlier.

'If you step outside for a few minutes, Mr Sims, I will settle your wife back in bed. She'll feel better then.'

The man presses one hand down on his salt and pepper head and then nods before handing a travel bag to the nurse. 'I've brought some things for her,' he says, giving Emma one last look before disappearing from the room.

The nurse turns back tutting. Within a few seconds, Paul reappears and helps his colleague sweep Emma up from the floor and back onto the mattress. As fast as he arrives, he leaves, and Emma is left alone with the nameless female nurse.

'Now let's get you tucked into bed, Mrs Sims. Then I'll get something to relax you.'

Emma pushes the nurse's hands away. 'I don't want to relax. I don't want to get back into this bed. And stop calling me that name.'

The nurse rests her spurned hands on her hips. 'Which name would that be? Mrs Sims?'

'Yes! Stop saying that.'

'What would you like to be called then?' There is a sarcastic tone to the question.

'Emma. Just call me by my name. I'm not missus anybody.'

The nurse rolls her eyes. 'Look, Dear, I'm not interested in your private affairs. Just your health.'

'Well, there's no need for you to be concerned about me. Look, I don't want to be here anymore. I want to go home.' It sounds childish but she doesn't care.

'Well, you're not ready to go home just yet. The doctor is coming around later, and he'll tell you when you can be discharged. Now try to get some rest. Your husband will come back tomorrow. Oh, and your daughter rang, too.'

Falling back onto the pillow, Emma places her hands over her face in despair. 'He is not my husband. I'm not married. I don't have a husband.'

'Now you're being silly,' the nurse says. 'You know full well you are married.'

'Don't tell me what I know,' Emma snaps. 'Why would I lie about something like that?'

The nurse rolls her eyes for the umpteenth time. She bends down and opens the drab bedside cabinet door. After some rummaging, she remerges holding a plastic bag which she tosses onto Emma's chest. 'I really don't have time for this, Mrs … Emma.'

'Why have you thrown this at me? What is it?' Emma picks up the bag to take a closer look. A few items of jewellery are just about visible through the barely transparent material – a watch, a necklace, earrings, and some rings. A gold band. Emma squints at the objects wondering what they have to do with her. Then the penny drops. 'Hey, I don't know whose jewellery this is, but it's certainly not mine. It's not even my style.'

The nurse snatches the bag back and pulls out the gold band. 'Never mind the rest of the jewellery. We took this off your finger when you were first admitted. It's been in here ever since. Are you satisfied?'

'That's not my ring. It must belong to another patient. They put it with me by mistake.'

'We'll try it for size, shall we?' the nurse says, reaching for Emma's finger.

Emma wrenches her hand from the nurse's grasp. 'Get off me!'

'Okay! There's no need for that.' The nurse replaces the bag closing the cabinet door firmly. 'Now let's get this bed tidied.'

'I'm sorry but listen. There's been a mix-up, a huge mistake. I have a boyfriend, but we're not married. At least, not yet. Wait! Where is he? Where's …' The name still won't come to her. She knows he is out there somewhere; she can feel it in her sinking heart.

The nurse's hands are slightly less gentle as she tidies the crumpled sheets once more. 'Where's who, Luvvie?' she asks, paying little attention. Judging by the change of tone, her mind has already moved on to the next patient.

But Emma hasn't moved on. In fact, she is getting more and more bewildered. She thinks it is almost comical the things she's heard in the last ten minutes or so. A husband she's never set eyes on before, and a daughter - who phoned. The people around her must be crazy or just ridiculously incompetent. Or both. Of course, that is the most rational explanation for all this surrealism. Everyone around her has made a huge mistake. Well, she would gladly accept that. She allows herself to breathe a wishful thinking sigh of relief.

'That's better,' the nurse says. 'Now I'll be back later.' Emma has other ideas.

'Wait! You mentioned a daughter. How old is this daughter?' Now the nurse will understand the mistake. How will she take it? She will probably laugh even though the whole thing is so terribly embarrassing.

The nurse shrugs. 'She didn't give her age, possibly because she was too concerned about her mother being in hospital.' The sarcastic tone has returned.

'But she telephoned the hospital herself, did she?' Emma is struggling to keep the composure that has returned to her.

By now the nurse is at the door. 'Yes, and like I just said, she is very worried about you.'

'About her twenty-three-year-old mother?' Emma can be sarcastic, too. She pauses. 'Yes, she must be a very able daughter to have done that all by herself.'

There is another, much longer pause before the nurse replies. 'Twenty what?' Her hand remains on the door handle. Emma can see that the nurse is considering what she's said but there is something about her expression that is not right. She is not laughing or cringing with embarrassment. An array of other emotions passes over her face. Horror, realisation, sympathy.

'What did you say?' The nurse has barely moved since hearing Emma's last statement.

'Twenty-three.' The muffled words come from behind Emma's hands. She didn't realise they were still covering her face when she spoke out. Her assertion, rather than confident and direct, must have been little more than a strangled plea. Did the stupid nurse even hear what she said? She removes her hands and shouts, 'I'm only twenty-three.'

The phrase finally hits its target like a tranquiliser dart. The nurse is apparently lost for words, yet it is her move, her turn to respond. Emma wonders what she's waiting for. At last, after what seems like an age, the nurse reaches into her trouser pocket and pulls out a silver object. She hands it to Emma who, after a moment of confusion, lifts it to her face.

There are no wrinkles on the tired-looking reflection in the mirror, just deep indents around the mouth. The skin surrounding the dull eyes is dark and the lids sag slightly. The matted brown hair is obviously dyed as silver strands are poking out around the temple. At the edges, the mouth droops as if reflecting the situation it finds itself in. It is not her face. At least, it is not her face as she knows it. She can see the familiar features: her round nose, greenish-brown eyes, and square chin. That tiny scar on her left eye socket caused by a garden swing. Also, there is the familiar worried expression, one which she can never alter whatever the occasion. And at this moment she is very worried. The nightmare is getting worse. This is the face of a middle-aged woman. This is her future face.

The blood races through her body, and she wonders if her heart can deal with the physical as well as the emotional trauma. What if she is having a heart attack? A crazy thought enters her mind. Is it true that you never die in a dream, that you always wake up before it happens? Wake up! Please wake up from this nightmare!

There is a gentle squeeze of her shoulder, and the frightening image disappears. 'Get some rest. You'll feel better after some sleep.' The nurse slips the tiny mirror back into her pocket. Her tone is kinder and more sympathetic, but Emma does not hear it. Nor does she see her leave the room. She no longer cares.

She can hear the faint sound of time ticking away. Emma assumes it is inside her head because there are no clocks or watches in sight. The metrical beats, hypnotic and strangely calming, give her time to reflect on the unbelievable situation she finds herself in. If that woman in the mirror really was her, if it wasn't a devious trick, she has aged years, decades in the blink of an eye. Because her last memory was being at a party, and Rosa was there too and they were both young.

The image is still fresh in her mind. The garden and the orange juice and the balloon. Her mum and dad. She can see them walking together as she called out to them. Just like she called out to Rosa. More tears well up in her washed-out eyes as she faces the inescapable truth. Not one of them noticed her. It was as if Emma wasn't really there. Or they weren't. This could only mean one thing. It was just a dream. A churning feeling is growing deep inside her. It could be nausea, hysteria, or both, but it is dwarfed by fatigue. She has no fight left. All she wants to do is go back to sleep, return to her dreams where she can be young again.

She pulls herself further onto the bed but a soft blunt noise on the floor catches her attention. Looking down she catches sight of a large brown object poking out from under the bed, a brown leather vanity case similar to one her mother has. Her heart misses a beat. Is it her mother's case? She needs to check. Sliding forward again she stretches out one foot to drag it closer. But when she tries to lift the bag, her leg merely shakes in response. It does not feel like the limb of a young athletic woman of twenty-three. But she keeps trying. At last, she manages to grab the handle with one hand and pull the bag up. The clasp is locked. It shouldn't bother her, but it does. She tosses the bag against the room in frustration. When it hits the wall, the contents spill out: various clothes, a toiletry bag, and a paperback book. And something shining against the drabness of the newly created heap. A golden glint appears to dart around as if someone were pointing a flashlight at Emma's eyes. Then she realises that she is the one moving thus creating the optical illusion. Unlike her, the mystery object is inanimate.

Curiosity gets the better of her, and she carefully lowers her body onto the floor. After crawling over to the untidy pile, she picks up what turns out to be a compact case. Her mother has one identical to this. Slowly, she pushes the golden clasp and watches as slivers of glass fall out onto her lap. As she brushes them off, she winces as one pierces her hand causing a short sharp sting. To think something so tiny could cause that much pain. But it is a pain that disappears in seconds. Her own fragmented image in the strewn shards is a far greater agony because it reflects an undeniable fact. There is no trick of the mind, no cruel joke. She can see the truth with her own eyes. The reflection shows that she is the same age as the man who claims to be her husband. She is old like him.

Taking the largest piece of glass, she eases herself back into bed and pulls the sheet over her. Then, after lying back, she drags the glass against her wrist.

CHAPTER THREE

The house is empty. She knows she should not go inside by herself, but even so, she steps forward and closes the beautiful oak front door behind her. It should not have been left unlocked because anyone could enter. The light is diminishing, and the far end of the hall is in darkness, but she is focussed on straight ahead. Without blinking she is halfway up the curved staircase. There is no sound coming from above or below not even from her own shoes pressing on the wooden treads. There is only an eerie silence. She feels her heart pounding inside her chest but isn't scared. If she can just reach the landing, things will become clearer. Three more steps. One, two, three. She hears something. Melodic singing drifts down the narrow corridor. It is coming from the furthest bedroom. She calls her mother and father despite knowing the sweet voice belongs to neither. Now it is laughing. Who is upstairs? A dark line appears on the landing wall increasing in size until a human shadow forms. A shiver runs down her spine and she wants to step backwards, however, her legs will not obey her mind's command. She shouldn't have gone into the house by herself.

***

The woman's voice remains pitch perfect as she sings along to whatever music is flowing through her earphones. Whether this is the intention or not, the earphones provide a barrier between her and the sedated patient, the one who is probably a bit too close for comfort. The location of the cleaner's Walkman is a mystery to Emma. Besides the fact that the radio itself is nowhere to be seen, there are no visible wires coming from the ridiculously large pink headphones. They must be hidden amongst the pink fur, she assumes. Or is it the strange light that is blurring so much detail? Not that it matters. The sun's rays squeezing through the partially opened blinds lend a kaleidoscopic tint to the drab hospital room. This colour gives the surroundings an interesting allure that is undeserved but welcome all the same.

Ignoring the stinging beneath her bandaged wrist, Emma scans the room for the thousandth time trying to spot anything unfamiliar to her, something that could not have been around in 1993. According to everyone she's asked, the year is 2023. That's right, 2023; a year that sounds straight out of a HG Wells novel. But if she really has travelled thirty years into the future, things would look different, wouldn't they? Everything would be constructed out of some twenty-first- century material, something that would not be out of place in a science fiction film. Shiny tinfoil or diamond-cut alloy steel. But there is nothing that stands out. The grey tiled flooring has a boring timeless look to it as does the high-back visitor's chair against the wall. The cold white cotton sheets and metal bedstead are barriers to comfort. But, however harsh and sterile, the furnishing is most welcome in its familiarity. She imagines it was no different in 1953.

For a few minutes, she allows a banished hope to creep back into her head - the idea that the whole thing is a bizarre trick, and she is still in 1993. It doesn't remain there long, however, because there are subtle differences - the nurses' uniforms for one. They are nothing like the starched blue and white dresses and white caps that they ought to be wearing. Nor do the doctors wear white coats, the ones that show they are the most important people in the hospital. In fact, she can't tell if someone is a nurse or a doctor. Or even a cleaner. They all look like actors in an American drama. Maybe that's it. Maybe she's in New York or Florida having been swept across the Atlantic Ocean. After all, her hair still smells of seaweed so she must have been in the sea a long time. The idea is fantastical, she knows, but less so than being transported into the future without stepping foot in a time machine. Another difference has been banished to the darkest regions of her mind. And to make sure it stays there, she has no intention of looking in a mirror again any time soon.

One of the more mundane things that haven't changed is the jug of water standing on the bedside table to her right, and at this moment, she is thirsty. There is something else to the right of her, something dark, but a blinding spasm hits her whenever she tries to look at it. It is probably nothing significant, but she wants to know what it is anyway because this is not the first time she's noticed it. Her attention returns to something she can see – the jug. She tries to shout out to the cleaner, but only silent words come out of her mouth, so Emma leans back and relaxes again. She can wait a while longer for water. Especially if she recently swam across the ocean.

The rhythmic motion of the buffer sweeping across the floor is hypnotic and she can feel her eyes growing heavy. Or is she asleep and the cleaner just a face in a dream? Her mind is so muddled that she can't even remember what she was doing with her life before waking up here. Did she finish university? Did she ever go to university? Was she clever enough? Some of her dreams seem to involve a celebration of some sort. Perhaps it was her graduation party. Yes, that would explain it. But deep down she knows it won't matter when she finally remembers the reason for the party. It won't change the fact that she is lying in a hospital bed sometime in the future. That she is now fifty-three years old, older than her own parents. Why does it matter about some stupid party?

Her muddled mind shifts in focus. The drugs they've given her have numbed the anguish that is still bubbling beneath her skin, and she closes her eyes. For the first time, she is able to dwell upon certain aspects of the nightmare without being overwhelmed by a wave of terror.

Something is buried deep inside her memory, and she cannot prise it out. That man with the grey in his hair. Perhaps she has seen him before. Despite her initial reaction when he first came into the room, there is something about him, a feeling perhaps, that is vaguely familiar. It's like watching a film and recognising one of the actors but there will be no credits at the end of this awful experience. She must try to remember who he is. He could be a friend of her father's. That would explain the generation gap. What was his name again? Simmons? Siddons?

'Emma Sims?'

The voice is faint and its precise location unidentifiable. Emma opens her eyes but can no longer see anything in the room. After an instinctive panic, she remembers this blindness has afflicted her several times before and will improve. Indeed, ten seconds or so pass and dark shapes are now visible. It seems the cleaner's outline is no longer there and has been replaced by another, one that is both taller and slimmer. Rather than swaying back and forth in the near distance, this new person stands much closer and completely motionless. The posture suggests he or she is a senior doctor, however, doctors, like nurses, are always on the move when away from the nursing station. It is rare to see them standing around not speaking. Emma wonders if she is hallucinating, and the person is not really there, a figment of her imagination or a trick of the light. She blinks a few times. The person is still there. Emma holds her breath, waiting for this new stranger to intrude into her life. Three, two, one.

'Mrs Sims, my name is Detective Sergeant Oliver Carr and I need to speak to you about the incident at the boathouse. Are you feeling ready to talk?'

The voice of the stranger is clearly male but it takes a while for Emma to comprehend his words. 'Pardon? Talk about what? Did you say you were a detective?'

'Yes. Detective Oliver Carr. I'd like your account of what happened at the boathouse in Seahaven. What do you remember, Mrs Sims?'

The same words. Nothing! Was that the same boathouse the other man mentioned, the one she has no memory of being at? Or is this just another part of the nightmare? Yes. Although the shape in front of her looks solid enough to be real, a nightmare makes far more sense. There would be an explanation for everything she is encountering. She must have been looking at a cruise brochure before ... before what?

'Mrs Sims, can you hear me?'

Mrs Sims! Emma is too tired to fight the battle again so soon. A blink of both eyes is taken as a nod.

'Can you tell me why you left the boathouse that night?'

No. I have no idea what you are talking about. 'I'm sorry but I don't remember.'

'Are you sure, Mrs Sims? It was only a few hours ago,' the detective says.

'A few hours?' Emma frowns. 'Have I only been in here a few hours?'

'Okay. I'm stretching the point a bit, but it's only been about forty-eight hours since the Seahaven boathouse incident. So, could you tell me everything you can remember about what happened there?'

'I'm sorry but I have no idea. Perhaps you could tell me what happened at the Seaway boathouse, Detective.'

The detective tuts. 'Seahaven. That's not the purpose of this conversation. I'm asking you for the answers, Mrs Sims. Not providing them myself.'

That name again. 'Well, if you won't tell me anything, we might as well stop right now because I've got nothing to say to you.'

'Please keep in mind that you are talking to a police officer.'

'Look, I'm not well. What makes you think you can just barge into a hospital room and pester a sick patient? There's not even a nurse or doctor with you. So, how do you know you've got the right person, officer?'

'We'll get to that in a moment. I'll repeat my own question. Why did you leave the boathouse?'

Somehow Emma allows herself to relax slightly and decides to be firm with the detective. She's had enough of him already. 'That wasn't your question actually. But for your information, I don't remember being at this boathouse you keep going on about. In fact, I've never been to a boathouse in my life. And I certainly didn't do a runner from one in the way you're suggesting.'

'Giving a false statement is an offence, Mrs Sims.'

'But it's true. You can ask anyone who knows me well. I have never set foot on a boat, or a ship and I've certainly never been in trouble. You can ask my parents.'

Detective Carr pauses and scans the small room as if for inspiration. Footsteps behind the door bring him back on track. 'Obviously, that is not correct, Mrs Sims.'

'What do you mean? Believe it or not, I know my own life.'

'I'm talking about the specifics, Mrs Sims. The boathouse and the ... well let's stick to the boathouse for now. You obviously were there.'

Emma is getting more and more irritated. The sedatives are beginning to wear off. 'Obvious to you maybe, but not to me. You could tell me I'd been to the moon and back and it would mean just as much.'

The footsteps have stopped.

'I think she needs more time to recover from this.' The man claiming to be her husband is in the room again, his face burning with rage. He is now acting as her protector. 'I'll thank you to leave this second.'

Carr shuffles his feet. 'Just a few more questions. And I'd like to speak to you too. It involves a cold case I know you're familiar with.'

'A cold case. Absolutely not!' he shouts. 'Have you not got anything better to do? No wonder the streets are so dangerous these days.'

'Please, Mr Sims.' The surprisingly youthful-sounding detective is clearly not intimidated by the man's fierce tone. 'A woman died.'

A woman died. 'Who's died? Is it my mother?' Emma's heart pounds in dread of the answer to her own question. But it seems no one has heard it.

The older man's tone changes. 'Oh, you mean, but that was thirty years ago, Detective. Why on earth are you bothering about this now?'

Thirty years ago. Emma's mind is in overdrive after hearing this. She wasn't even born thirty years ago. So, they must have mistaken her for another woman, the real Mrs Sims. Perhaps she left him, and he is unable to face the reality of being without her. Yes, that explains everything. If they would just shut up, she could tell that policeman what's happened. But Emma finds herself a spectator in this stalemate: two strangers arguing about another stranger. No names are mentioned but Emma is relieved as it allows her to continue with her reassuring theory and she is happy for this to continue. But of course, it eventually ends because the disturbance has caught the attention of a passing nurse.

'What's going on here?' the nurse says, directing her irritation at the visitors. 'Mrs Sims is suffering from an extreme case of amnesia. She is very distressed.'

'This won't take much time,' Carr insists, still addressing the other man.

But the nurse is adamant. 'Not now, Detective. This should wait until the doctors have okayed it.'

Carr raises his hands in the air. 'Fair enough. I can speak to her again.' He takes what appears to be a notebook out of his pocket. 'Perhaps you could give me your account of the evening, Mr Sims.'

This seems to have taken the other man by surprise. He turns his head towards Emma before looking back to the detective. 'Whatever for? Unless I'm very much mistaken, having an accident is not illegal.'

'That would depend on the circumstances surrounding the accident,' Carr replies.

'What utter nonsense you are talking! Are you suggesting I threw my wife into the middle of the ocean?'

'There's no need to be flippant. This is a serious investigation. Did you notice any strangers at your party, someone not on the guest list?'

'Wait. What stranger? Are you here about a cold case or some mystery gate crasher?'

'There is a connection between the two, Mr Sims. If you could just remember seeing any unknown faces.'

His voice fades as he considers the question. 'Who do you have in mind, Detective? Is there something we should know?'

'I'm the person who wants to know,' Carr replies defiantly. 'A young woman went to the boathouse on Saturday with the intention of speaking to Mrs Sims. I'd like to hear what she has to say about that.'

'A young woman wanted to speak to Emma. Are you telling me you've intruded on my wife's recovery to talk about that? This is absurd.'

'Well, there is more to it than that but I'm not at liberty to discuss it with you yet.'

'Well, come back when you are, detective. But not here, obviously. In fact, I intend to speak to your superiors about this.'

'I understand this isn't ideal, but it's been extremely difficult to reach your wife before now. I tried visiting the house on numerous occasions, but the door was never opened.'

'To talk about this young woman?'

'No. At the time I was calling about the cold case. However, now I would like information about the young woman who talked to your wife at the boathouse.'

'Are you deliberately trying to confuse us?'

The detective tuts. 'Oh come now, Mr Sims. I'm sure you of all people are more than capable of keeping up with this.'

'Not while I'm dealing with my wife's recovery.' He takes a deep breath before continuing. 'Look call around the house later and we can discuss this then.'

'As I've already said, I've tried that on numerous occasions but with no luck.'

'This time I'll be there to speak to you. My wife never answers the door to strange men.'

'I need to speak to Mrs Sims more than you. You were interviewed at the time about the death of ...'

'Look, that's quite enough for now.'

'I'll be the judge of that, Mr Sims,' the detective says, keeping his head fixed on the notebook he is holding in his hand.

This seems to tip Mr Sims over the edge. 'I know my wife's rights, even if you are trying to trample all over them.'

The detective turns his back on Emma. 'I have a very good reason to be here. Unfortunately, I'm not at liberty to disclose all of the details at this time but you can rest assured you'll be informed very shortly. That reason in itself takes precedence over your wife's rights.'

'You're wrong, Detective. So, get out of that kangaroo court you keep in your head.' His voice is sharp but controlled. 'And while you're at it, get out of here.'

An uncomfortable atmosphere falls over the small room. It is as though both combatants are deciding their next move. The detective is the one to break the silence. 'I'll put the aggressive manner down to stress, Mr Sims. Next time I would advise you to be more forthcoming about this serious investigation. Good day.' He marches out of the room without acknowledging the patient he initially came in to interview.

The man turns to Emma but sees she has fallen asleep. For several minutes he paces up and down as far as the room's small dimensions will allow. At last, he charges through the door, and Emma opens her eyes. She needs to think.

CHAPTER FOUR

She is walking down a battered corridor. There is no sound, not even of her black leather shoes on the vinyl tiles. At first, she thinks she is alone but then sees a towering figure in front of her, his long black cape floating behind him. She is trailing him but struggles to keep up with his giant strides. An ugly door, half glass half wood, is push opened, and she follows him through it. Now it is as if a sound button has been pressed and she hears him muttering indecipherable words to a mousy woman standing at the front of the classroom. Thirty pairs of bright eyes fix on her, and she wants to die on the spot. Giggles, smirks and nudges. The adults either miss or choose to ignore the scraps of paper being passed under the desks. The woman's mouth is moving, but nothing audible comes out. The half-glass door opens and closes again. The tall man is no longer there. The woman stretches her arm out then returns to the blackboard. Emma, her heart sinking, walks towards the empty desk and sits down. The girl sitting next to her pokes out her tongue. The boy in front makes a raspberry sound. There is a hiss. She turns to look at the girl behind her. She is pretty with red tousled curls and dark blue eyes. She winks. *Don't worry. It'll be all right. I'll take care of you.*

***

Emma sleeps well and her vision is much clearer than it has been since she first woke up in hospital. She is getting used to the hard mattress and inflexible bedding, and it is beginning to feel like her own bed. If only she could say the same about the room itself which is sterile and ugly, nothing like her own bedroom. Her own bedroom? A shiver runs through her as she thinks of the man who calls himself her husband and his wild allegations. Perhaps it would be better to move into a ward with other patients where she would never be alone with him. Yes, she'll ask the nurse if she could be moved as soon as possible. She spends the next twenty minutes rehearsing a conversation in her mind with each of the various nurses who are around today. Out of all of them, she would prefer Paul as he is the only nurse who makes time to sit with her. And the only one whose name she knows. Yes, she'll ask Paul.

But it's another unfamiliar face that walks through the door next, not one of the nurses. This woman doesn't look like hospital staff, dressed as she is in dark jeans and a rather unflattering burgundy sweatshirt. No. She is neither a doctor nor a nurse. There is no expensive shirt and tie, no boiler suit of any colour, no constant checking of a timepiece. At first, Emma thinks it is another detective back to question her about things she knows nothing: a young woman, a mystery boathouse and a person who died years ago. But the last detective seemed suspicious, impatient, angry even, while this latest visitor shows no emotion on her pleasant face.

'Hello, Emma. Do you mind if I call you that?' Her tone is bright while her lips remain firmly horizontal.

Emma looks at her with suspicion. The very fact that the woman calls her by her first name before asking if she minds should annoy her, yet it doesn't. Whoever this woman is, Emma thinks, she has clearly been informed of her reaction to being called Mrs Simpson or whatever it was. And this has an immediate positive effect. Also, there is something strangely calming about the woman's manner. It is a welcome change that any such thoughts and feelings there may be, remain hidden behind the woman's passive expression. No relief, no sorrow, no anger. Yes, it is a welcome change even if Emma isn't quite sure how to take it. But this time she will try to stay calm.

'Emma is my name so that's fine.' Then trying to get the upper hand, she adds, 'What is your name?'

'I'm Mandy and I work here part-time. How are you feeling right now? I've heard about how upset you were earlier.'

Brushing her shortish dark blonde hair back as far as it will go, she fiddles with the pencil which is wedged behind one ear. 'Is it all right, if I sit here?'

Emma continues her own questioning. 'Are you a psychiatrist? Do you think I'm mad?'

'No, and no. Besides, mad is not a word I tend to use to describe anybody.' There is no hint of a rebuke in her voice.

'But that's what you do think, or you wouldn't be walking on eggshells right now,' Emma continues, feeling strangely empowered by the other woman's rather shabby image.

'Is that how I seem to you? Because I can assure you, I am perfectly relaxed.' She is now sitting on the visitors' chair, scribbling something in a notebook.

Silence descends on the room apart from the gentle flapping of blinds against the windowpane. The sound is remarkably soothing. A memory comes to Emma of school lessons in the summer term just before the holidays began. She can see her teacher now, staring out of the window as much as any one of the pupils, mentally packing his case for the well-deserved long holiday. Those six weeks seemed like an eternity to children and young teenagers; the university break was even longer. Yes, she did go to university. But what did she study? It was not so long ago. She closes her eyes, but it doesn't help.

The sound of paper fluttering in the breeze brings her back to the hospital room. The other woman is still there scribbling away. Emma is bemused by her latest visitor who has yet to announce the purpose of her presence. Perhaps she just needed somewhere to sit down and write in her notebook. What did she say her name was? Mary, she thinks. Why can she remember that but not what she studied at university? After all, it wasn't so long ago. But it will come back to her. It must.

The rustling of paper continues. Emma wonders what she is supposed to say to this person who obviously has some role to justify. Perhaps she is somebody's secretary, the psychiatrist's secretary maybe. That would explain the pencil. She is probably using shorthand which she will type up later. Still silence. Emma can bear it no longer. 'What are you writing?'

Mandy looks up. 'Ah, just a to-do list for later. Sorry about this.' She continues writing for a short while longer before finally closing the book. 'Now you've got my full attention.'

Emma gives her a puzzled look. 'What do you mean? I didn't ask you to come here.' She realises how defensive the comments sound before the last word leaves her mouth, but it is too late. She's been trying to express a placidness she doesn't feel, hiding the anxiety and panic wrestling to get out.

It is laughable to try but it gives her a chance to work out her next move. Too many strangers are telling her things about herself that she doesn't recognise. One person appears and then another immediately after. It is like an assault course that gives her no chance to take stock of the nightmare situation, to untangle the spaghetti in her mind. But she knows she needs to keep trying so manages to feign composure. 'I'm sorry, Mary. My head is banging through lack of sleep, but I shouldn't take it out on you.'

'Mandy. Don't apologise, Emma. That's the last thing you need to worry about. I hope I can be of some help to you, someone you can talk to.' She looks at her watch. 'Everybody tells me I'm a good listener. Why don't you give me a try?'

Emma thinks it is an odd way to speak, a bit informal for a stranger, but finds herself responding openly. 'To be honest everything is still a haze. There are so many things I can't remember, and I don't know why I'm in hospital.' The mask of composure slips down, and she begins to cry. 'I don't recognise anyone who comes in. Every name I hear means nothing to me. And I can't remember what I did at university.' The tears are now uncontrollable.

After passing Emma a tissue, Mandy offers words of compassion despite maintaining her blank expression. 'Look, I can see you are upset, so why don't you tell me what you do know?'

Emma sighs. 'That's just it. I don't know anything anymore. All I do is lie here trying to make sense of my life, but I can't do that if I don't remember it.'

'Try again, Emma. Close your eyes if you like. Sometimes, that helps.'

Close your eyes. That was the start of it. 'Okay. When I closed my eyes, I was a young woman. Then when I opened them again, I was over fifty years old and ...' she gasps before continuing, 'and I still am. That is all I know and remember. I bet you think that's mad, right? A real joke.'

But Mandy does not laugh. 'So, where were you when you closed your eyes?'

Emma opens her mouth but realises she cannot answer the question. 'Er, I, um ... wait ... I know I was at a big party. It was my dad's, I think, his fiftieth. No, wait, he's not that old. Hang on. Maybe it was my mum's.'

'That sounds more than possible. Is your mum fifty?'

'No, my mother isn't fifty either. It must have been for something else. A special occasion, maybe.' Her head is swimming. Why can't she remember? She can see the number two on the balloon. What is the other number? If only she could see it.

'Okay. So, the party isn't for your mother or your father, or at least not a fiftieth birthday party. We can rule that one out. Is anyone else at this party apart from you and your parents?'

Emma pictures the orange juice on the garden table. 'Rosa. Yes, Rosa was there.'

'Who is Rosa?'

'Rosa is my friend, my best friend. We are more like sisters than anything. As a matter of fact, I'm worried about her, why she hasn't been to visit me.'

'Perhaps she doesn't know you are here.'

Emma looks at Mandy as if the woman has two heads. 'Of course, she would know I'm here. We were all together.'

'Together where?'

'At the party, of course. Isn't that what we've been talking about?' Emma reminds herself not to lose control.

'Okay. What is Rosa's surname? I could see if she's called the hospital.'

At last. 'It's Rosa ... um...' She closes her eyes, but it doesn't help. *Her best friend. Like sisters.* 'It'll come to me in a minute.'

'That's fine. At this party, the one we've been discussing, did you go to bed as normal?'

'What do you mean by normal?' Emma asks.

'Well, you tell me what normal is to start with. What time do you usually go to bed for instance?'

'The same time everyone goes,' Emma replies, accepting she has no idea. 'Later at the weekend, of course.'

'And what time did you go to bed the night of the party, Emma?'

'I don't remember. There would have been a lot of drinking, I suppose.'

'Did you go to bed at home or somewhere else?'

Emma squeezes her hands together trying desperately to remember where she was before waking up in this nightmare. But she can't. The more she thinks about it, the more she realises she couldn't have been in bed, or she wouldn't be all alone in hospital. Her family and friends would know she was here. Yet someone must have called the ambulance. Was it her mother? Her father? Rosa?

'Emma?' Mandy is still expressionless. 'Where were you when you closed your eyes before waking up as the person you are now?'

After considering the question, Emma shakes her head in frustration. 'Okay. I didn't exactly close my eyes. It was a figure of speech.'

'Does that mean your age didn't double in the blink of an eye?' Her voice is kind if slightly mocking.

'Yes. No. Look, I'm confusing myself. I wasn't in bed at all. I was awake, not asleep. It's just I don't know why I was there and now I'm here.'

'And where was "there"?'

Emma tries to unravel the meaning of Mandy's simple question before deciding it would get her nowhere. She sighs and, shaking her head, returns to the only image she has. 'In a garden, my parents' garden. And Rosa was there, and she looked just like she was when I last saw her.'

'What do you mean by that? Didn't you last see her at the party? Is your last memory of that garden scene?' Mandy's attention is on her notes as she asks the three questions, her eyes hidden from view.

More silence while Emma grasps around her mind for clarity. There is none. When she was in the garden it was daytime and before the party started. That's if there even was a party. A hard lump forms in her throat but she fights against the self-doubt. 'Well, what about my parents? They were both young in my ...'

'In your what, Emma?'

She closes her eyes and repeats the question to herself. Was it a memory or just a dream? Then scratching at her knuckles, she asks the question she is no longer sure she wants to know the answer to. 'Where are they? Where are my parents?'

Now Mandy shakes her head. Whether the gesture means that she doesn't know, or that she doesn't want to say isn't clear. Emma chooses not to ask for clarification because she feels she isn't prepared for all the possible answers.

'Why don't you tell me more about your friend? Her life and her family,' Mandy says.

Emma is confused. 'Why do you want to know about her? What's her life got to do with this?'

'Perhaps talking about your friend will help your memory settle. Tell me about Rosa. Where does she live?'

To Emma, it seems crazy but at least she can focus on someone else rather than herself. And Rosa is the one person still clear in her mind's eye. 'London. At least she did live there. I'm not sure now. That doesn't make any sense, does it?'

'What makes you say that, Emma?'

'Because I should know exactly where she lives if we're so close.'

'How do you know her?'

'When I joined her school, I was shy and terrified but she took me under her wing. We became inseparable and couldn't imagine a world without each other. It was like we were one person sharing likes and dislikes, moods and feelings, thoughts and dreams.'

'That sounds like a special friendship, Emma.'

'It was precious.' Immediately she sighs. 'Why did I say "was"?'

'Are you and Rosa no longer close?'

'I don't know. Why do you think that is?'

'Why did Rosa move to London?' Mandy asks, ignoring Emma's question.

'She got into this drama college. Rosa was always in the school plays and usually the star of the show. People use to make fun of her, saying she was embarrassing herself. Some girls were really cruel and joked that Rosa had to pretend to be someone else because her own life was so awful. But she had the last laugh because the experience at school really brought out her talent. She developed all these emotional sounds and expressions to the point where even I didn't know which ones were genuine.'

'And *was* her life awful?'

'What?'

Mandy bends her head to one side. 'Why did those girls say Rosa had an awful life?'

Emma thinks for a few seconds but knows the answer to that question is not available to her yet. 'Those girls were mean and would say anything. I was Rosa's only friend.' She wants to say that she still is but something is stopping her. 'But she was better than all of them.'

'So, she's an actress. Has she been on television?'

'Not television, no, but she's been on stage in the West End, at least in the smaller theatres.'

'Impressive. Did you ever go to see her?'

Did she? 'I don't remember.' Yet another part of her life a blank. Emma closes her eyes to absorb her own words. 'I guess we were growing apart.'

Crockery clinks beyond the door destroying the silence of the past few seconds. Emma looks across at the expressionless woman who is finally receiving the answer to a question asked some time ago.

'I think I may have argued with Rosa. We may have had a fight or something. Perhaps she's here too, in this very hospital as a patient. Could you check? You wouldn't need her full name to do that. She's got red wavy hair and she's really pretty. Please check to see if she's here.'

'Of course, I will.'

She glances at Mandy's pencil, but it remains flat on her lap. There is a whirring sound beyond the door, and it breaks her chain of thought. 'Can you tell me how I ended up here ... in hospital, I mean?'

'You were in the sea, Emma. Didn't your hus ... the doctor tell you?'

Emma stares at the other woman. 'You were about to say husband, weren't you? Do you know him? I mean, do you know without a doubt that he is my husband?'

'No, I don't know him at all to be quite honest.'

'So, you can't say that he is definitely my husband.'

'No, I haven't seen any documents. But why would he pretend to be someone he's not?'

'I have no idea. Maybe he's a conman or a ... a kidnapper.' She knows how ridiculous she is sounding. 'But whatever he has said about me, it is not true. It is a lie.'

'What has he said about you that's untrue, Emma?'

'Well, everything because he doesn't know me or anything about me so it would all be plucked from his imagination. How can he be my husband when I've never set eyes on him before this hospital?'

'Why, Emma? Surely he'd be taking a risk if he knew it was a lie, that he wasn't your husband. I mean he'd be lying right in front of you of all people.'

'But he already has, hasn't he? Lie after lie, in front of me, the doctors, the nurses, even that detective.'

'Detective?'

'Yes, the detective who came to see me here.'

Mandy makes some notes. 'What did he want?'

'He wasn't here long because that man got rid of him. He obviously didn't want me to speak to him for some reason. But when he appeared in the room, the detective asked me about a boathouse I didn't know and some young woman I didn't know either.'

Mandy puts down her pencil. 'That would be the boathouse you disappeared from Emma.'

Emma groans. 'Not you as well. I don't recall being at any boathouse let alone going to a party there.'

'That is something that I can confirm did happen. It is true, Emma. You were celebrating your twenty-fifth wedding anniversary at the Seahaven boathouse.'

Twenty-fifth wedding anniversary. The words sting like a thousand wasps and Emma wants to scream.

Mandy continues. 'You disappeared from the boathouse hours before being rescued from the sea.'

The sensation of waves bashing her freezing body overcomes Emma. 'The sea. Yes, I remember being in the sea, but I don't understand why I was there.' She stares at Mandy. 'Can you tell me why I was in the sea?'

The other woman shakes her head. 'Only you know why, Emma. A search and rescue helicopter pulled you out of the water after you were seen floating several miles away from the boathouse.'

'Several miles. That doesn't make any sense. I must have been kidnapped, taken out in a boat, and then dumped in the water. Wait! The detective. He came here alone without any member of staff.'

'I haven't heard anything about a detective, Emma. Perhaps you dreamt it.'

'No! One of the nurses spoke to him, too. At first, I thought he may be here to rescue me, sent by my parents or ... my boyfriend. But what if he was just pretending to be a detective? What if he abducted me and somehow I escaped.' She breathes out slowly. Her words are dispassionate as if spoken about a character in a murder mystery film that she could switch off at any time. Just like in the past. But this is no longer the past. Nor is it a film. This situation is horribly real. She looks down at her hands, focussing on the unfamiliar tough skin with its brown patches and crinkles on the knuckles. They are hands that are as unrecognisable as her face. They are indisputably middle-aged hands. Nothing is how it used to be. The tears come back, and another tissue is passed to her. After wiping her sodden face she asks, 'Have I been in a coma?'

The response is almost robotic. 'Not a coma, no. You have been recovering from a serious accident. There is no doubt the event was traumatic and may have caused some kind of amnesia. You need to be patient, Emma.'

'Amnesia.' It's such a small dulcet word for the ferocious earth-quake that has annihilated her life. 'Have I really got that?'

'Perhaps.'

Both women sit in silence their thoughts a world apart. Then Mandy looks at her watch before standing up. 'They are bringing around lunch, so I'd better leave.'

By the time Emma has refocussed, Mandy is already by the door. 'You will check your records, won't you?' she calls out.

Mandy turns around. For the first time, there is a hint of something in her eyes. But she quickly recovers. 'Oh yes. I'll do that now. Bye, Emma.'

CHAPTER FIVE

Once again they are in the garden, but this time there are no marquees, no balloons, no orange juice. It is a different period of her life. It is much earlier. A yellow paddling pool sprawls out over the lawn, its ugly plastic casing ruining the luxurious green turf. Howls and screams of delight cut through the hot sticky air as the girls splash each other with cool water. While Rosa is wearing a bikini which shows off her growing curves, Emma has a full swimming costume on, a childish one she has yet to grow out of. Her body still lacks the shape that puberty brings to all teenage girls eventually. The sun is directly above, yet her skin is hard and rough from the unwelcome goosebumps creeping down her arms. She wants to go inside and play music but knows Rosa is avoiding meeting her eye for this reason. She doesn't have a garden of her own so always wants to make the most of being in theirs. Emma's parents are in the garden too, but Rosa seems oblivious of everyone except herself. Emma can feel her body boiling with rage and tells her parents to go away. They both look hurt and rush back inside the house. Now she is racked with guilt. She calls after them, but it is too late. They can no longer hear her.

***

The pillow is damp, and Emma knows she has been crying in her sleep. This does not surprise her as she's been crying a lot lately. She cries while awake but more during the times her thoughts are beyond her control. It must be the dreams she has every night. Or are they memories? If only her mind wasn't so muddled, she could attempt to analyse the images and events playing out in her dreams. If only she could think straight. But for now, she must retune her mind to the current situation, the one that no longer appears to be a dream.

No one has told her if Rosa is also a patient at the hospital, or even if she's visited. The woman named Mandy was no use at all. Perhaps she was another mental patient. She hasn't dared ask the staff about her parents again. There is no way she could do so without a procession of red flags marching over her bed. How could she not know if her parents were alive or dead? She presumes they are dead, of course. And that is the most important reason for not asking – she doesn't want to know for sure.

But there are other people whose fate she could just about deal with. Rosa for one. She was in the garden along with Emma's parents. They were all together, enjoying the long summer days. But these thoughts take her back to square one. She can't be certain if the dream fragments are moments in time, flashbacks of actual situations, or merely the imagination of her battered mind. Sometimes, she experiences them while she is quite awake so they can't all be dreams. Which ones are fact, and which are fiction? She has no idea. Perhaps they are all the delusions of a crazy woman.

She's been lying in this bed for days. It isn't as though she's suffering from any obvious sickness or injury, at least not since that terrible headache when she first woke up. So each hour is seeming longer. Boredom is beginning to take precedence over the fear and panic that has gripped her since waking up in hospital. If only she had other patients to chat to. She stares at the door willing it to open, intent on demanding to be moved to a ward. Even if it's Dr Syed who walks through first.

However, the next person to enter the room is neither a nurse nor a visitor. The rattling of cups and squealing of rubber on Lino signal the arrival of the mid-morning cuppa, one of the valuable breaks in the long day. Emma spends the next few minutes pondering over her choice of hot beverage. Should she plump for coffee or tea? Will there be a better selection of biscuits than the previous day's custard cream and malted milk? The door opens with a bang as the trolley emerges first followed by a petite female in her early twenties.

'Good morning, Sweetheart,' the young woman says, without a hint of irony. 'What can I get you?'

'Good morning. Coffee, please. Milk no sugar.' Emma likes the cheerfulness of so many of the non-medical workers, each one coming in, doing their job well, then leaving again. In between they often chat to her about mundane topics like the weather or the passing of time. Not one of them pries or, even if they do, try to do so subtly. They don't act as if they have a right to know her business.

'Do you want me to put it down here,' the younger woman says, leaning towards the visitor's chair. 'It'll be less likely to spill, and it's very hot.'

'But I won't be able to reach it,' Emma says, trying not to sound ungrateful.

'Do you need a hand getting out of bed? The nurses are mad busy this morning, so they probably won't be in here for a bit.'

Emma wasn't expecting that. Her instinct is to refuse, but it is such a kind offer she can only smile and nod. Pulling back the sheets, she drapes her arm over the woman's delicate shoulder and, reminding herself she's a patient rather than a geriatric woman, allows herself to be guided into the chair. It is surprisingly comfortable, and she relaxes after picking up her cup and saucer. 'Thank you. I feel better sitting here,' she says, forcing herself not to wince after tasting the coffee. Did she ask for tea by mistake?

'No worries. Malted milk or custard cream?'

'Malted milk, please. You're very kind. What's your name?'

'Tina. Tina, the trolley girl.'

Emma gives a rare smile. 'Tina. That was my grandmother's name. What's the weather like today, Tina?'

'Well, it was drizzly when I came in at seven. They say it's gonna get heavier this afternoon. All the visitors will bring the rain in with them, so the floor will be soaking wet.' She shakes her head in disapproval.

'Do you take tea around all of the hospital?' Emma asks, no longer interested in the weather.

Tina laughs. 'You must be joking. I wouldn't get back in time for the patients' next meal. No. I just do this floor and the one below.'

'Oh. How many floors are there?'

'Six. Why do you ask? Thinking of going for a wander?'

Emma assumes that is a joke, so she smiles. 'Well, I was wondering if there were any spare beds. It would make a change to be on a ward with other patients, a bit of company at least.'

'You'd have to do more than move wards, Luv. There are no wards as such in this hospital. All the patients are in single rooms, not just you.'

'Oh, really. Does that mean everyone here is very sick?' All of a sudden, Emma feels faint.

But Tina laughs. 'Goodness, no. At least not everyone. This hospital was built that way for some reason. I guess it's not all bad. After all, you've got your own ensuite, haven't you.' She nods towards something out of Emma's view.

Ensuite? Emma is mystified not only by the knowledge she has her own bathroom but the realisation that she hasn't used it. Or has she? But it's a trivial matter she can't think about right now. 'Have you noticed a patient here, a woman with red curly hair? Her name is Rosa.'

Tina's eyes look to the ceiling. 'Let me see. Yes, the woman I served first this morning on the floor below ... she has reddish hair. Not sure if it's curly ... maybe wavy.'

'What's her name?'

'Don't know, sorry. I don't think she knows it right now either.
Poor thing's usually half asleep.'

Emma can't contain her excitement. It must be Rosa and she's
still recovering. That would explain why she hasn't been to see her.
'This woman ... is she pretty?' she shouts.

'Aw, yes. She's a dear. Anyway, I must be off. I'll see you tomorrow. Enjoy your tea, Luv.' She grabs the trolley and trundles back
out through the door.

'Wait,' Emma calls out to the closed door. She didn't get the
chance to send a message to Rosa.

Time passes by. Staff come and go. Emma is still sitting in the
visitor's chair aware that it is the first sign of acceptance. While
bedbound she was helpless, and dependent on others for eating,
washing and toileting. Like a baby. It was demeaning but she
hadn't cared because it allowed her to reject the world around her.
Now she could use the mysterious ensuite bathroom or walk away
if she wanted to. Leave the hospital, get on a bus, and go home.
She's taken the first steps, all three of them. The problem is that
she has no money for the bus fare. And that is a major problem.
But even if she could borrow the fare from Tina, she is no longer
sure where home is. So, Emma has accepted that for now there is
no escape. She has to adjust to the terrible bubble she is in. She
looks across at the door and realises she hasn't stepped beyond it.

Thinking of going for a wander? Perhaps she should.

A small group of medical staff are huddled around the nurses' station engrossed in some x-ray. Emma is surprised that not one of them looks at her as she shuffles past in the pink dressing gown she wouldn't normally be seen dead in. Maybe she is dead and that's why they don't look up; she is invisible. But shortly after moving away from the group, it is clear she is still very much alive.

The way ahead is a wide corridor which separates a line of individual rooms. Inside each room is a solitary patient. Some patients are asleep. Some are awake and reading. Some stare into their thoughts. A few lock eyes with her as she intrudes fleetingly into their personal ordeals. Male and female, most are elderly, but none appear to be in the last throes of life. Yet there are so many who look well over the age her grandparents reached. Both grandfathers passed away before seventy. Her two grandmothers lived longer but neither made it to eighty. Life expectancy must have risen in the current world. It is one positive, at least. Even if Emma is in her fifties, both her parents could still be alive and well as they were young having her. The thought distracts her and while walking blindly, her slippers kick something hard. Her toe hurts and she cannot help but curse the large yellow plastic bin that she should have noticed was there.

'Hello, Dear.' The voice is frail but somehow carries the short distance to the corridor. Its owner is staring at Emma.

'Oh, hello. Do you need anything?' Emma limps into the elderly woman's cubicle ready to offer her services. It would make a change to do something useful and she is perfectly capable of pouring water and plumping up pillows. She would draw the line at anything related to bedpans, however.

'It's Emily, isn't it?' The rising intonation suggests it is more a statement than a question.

'Er, yes. Emma.' Emma analyses the individual characteristics behind the generic wrinkly face. She half recognises the sparkling blue eyes looking back at her, but she needs more to go on. 'I'm sorry but my memory hasn't been right since my accident. Do you mind if I ask how it is you know me?'

The elderly woman seems surprised rather than offended. 'We lived next door to each other, well as near to being neighbours as anyone is out there.' The wrinkles fall away, and the face is transformed into that of Mrs Weekes, the woman across the lane from Emma's parents' house.

'Mrs Weekes,' Emma says. 'I can't believe it. Is it really you?'

'Of course, it's me. I suppose it's not so unbelievable that a woman of my age is in hospital. But oh, my dear, whatever's happened to you?' she says as if Emma had cut her knee.

At this display of kindness, Emma bursts into tears. Then not wanting the nurses to see her, she closes the door and sits down. 'I'm sorry. All I seem to do lately is cry. Things have been a bit rough these last few days. How are you, anyway? I hope you're not too unwell.'

Mrs Weekes smiles. 'Don't worry about me. Hopefully, I won't be here much longer. This is all Philip's doing. I only need to have a niggle and he calls an ambulance.'

Although she knows Mrs Weekes, Emma does not recognise the name Philip, but she assumes he is the son rather than the husband.

Perhaps she will get to meet him, too. 'You are looking well. Have they said when you can go home?'

She tuts. 'They say I can't look after myself. Who do they think has been looking after me for the past twenty years? Me that's who. Just because my blood pressure's a little low. It's better than being high, isn't it?'

Emma finds herself laughing. She doesn't know much about blood pressure because she's never had to worry about it. Not even her mother and father talked about such things as they were only ... 'It's good that you are so independent, Mrs Weekes. Does Philip help with things?'

'With his knees, he can barely help himself, poor lad. I suppose he could do without having me to worry about.'

Oh, he couldn't, Emma thinks. Aware that the other woman would probably know about her parents, she toys with the idea of mentioning them. It is the natural thing to do, after all, and she would regret it if she didn't. This might be her only opportunity. She prepares herself for the terrible confirmation of the fears that she's pushed to the back of her mind. 'Mrs Weekes, how long has it been since you last saw Mum and Dad?'

The older woman's smile drops, and her eyes grow dimmer as she considers the question. 'Oh, well, I suppose that would be at the funeral. Yes, of course, it was.'

At the funeral. Emma wonders why she isn't screaming. Perhaps she has no energy left for anything but a whisper. 'My mother's funeral?'

Now the older woman looks worried. 'Oh, dear. I didn't know Jennifer had passed away, too. When did that happen?'

It is a rare moment of relief quickly followed by the severest of emotional pain. Emma thinks it is clear whom she meant by *too*. But there would be more than enough time to grieve so she doesn't let herself get sidetracked. 'Was I there ... at the funeral?'

Mrs Weekes frowns again. 'What a strange question! You should know if you were there or not.'

'The problem is, Mrs Weekes, I'm having trouble remembering so many things. That's why I'm here. They think it may be some form of dementia.' As she says the word, Emma realises it may not be far from the truth.

'Oh no. You poor thing, and with you being so young as well. I thought you'd recovered from that, but then again ... Is it hereditary?'

Recovered. Hereditary. Emma wishes she had a notebook to jot down all the phrases that are baffling her because she doubts her befuddled mind will store them for long. Never mind. Whatever it is, she'll just have to deal with it. 'So, was I at the funeral, Mrs Weekes?'

'Well, of course. Why wouldn't ... Oh wait? Ah, it wasn't long after... Oh, dear.' The woman shakes her head as if cross with herself. 'No, you wouldn't have been there.'

'Why not? Where was I?' She has no memory of the funeral because she wasn't there. A mixture of confusion and relief seeps through her. Does Mrs Weekes even know whose funeral it was? Perhaps the elderly lady's memory is as faulty as hers, and she was talking about someone completely different. But no. She mentioned her mother's name. There is no escaping the horrible truth. 'Wait! You said not long after. Not long after what?'

'Gosh you are having problems with your memory, aren't you, Dear? After all this time, too.'

Emma needs to stop herself from grabbing the other patient by her shoulders and shaking the answers out of her. 'Please tell me why I wasn't at my father's funeral.'

'Not your father's funeral, Dear.'

Instant relief. Maybe her father isn't dead, at least not definitely. She can still hope to see him again. Then dread creeps back inside her because Mrs Weekes did not look so surprised this time.

Not your father's funeral.

Emma knows she should press further but self-preservation takes over in the form of a slight change of subject. Whomever Mrs Weekes is talking about, at least it's not either of her parents. 'Then whose, Mrs Weekes? Whose funeral was it?'

'Your friend's, Dear.'

A friend. Who was it? It couldn't be, could it? She must know. 'Mrs Weekes, which friend?'

The woman closes her eyes and nods to herself. 'I think her name was Rose or Rosie. No, it was Rosa.'

Emma thought the nightmare couldn't get any worse, but a nightmare does not sum up the horror of what she is experiencing. Every revelation is a dagger through her heart, physical and emotional agony so intense she doesn't understand how she is still breathing. Or maybe she isn't. If Hell is a place on Earth, surely, she is smack bang in the centre. Mrs Weekes has finally delivered the torture, news too terrible to respond to. Now after the terrible revelation, Emma sits in a stupor ignoring the patient whose bed she is sitting beside.

The brief reunion ends with the already familiar clanking of a machine being wheeled into their small space.

'Hello, girls. Glad you managed to get out of that room, sweetheart,' Tina says, as she collects the teacup next to Mrs Weekes. She tuts as she looks at the untouched contents. 'Forgot about it, did you, Luv?' Leaving two biscuits on the side table, and the two women with their thoughts, she trundles out of the room.

Mrs Weekes' eyes are closed. The intensity of the conversation has taken its toll on her tired mind, and her chest is rising and dropping with the irregularity that comes with fitful sleep. Emma wonders if she is dreaming of the past as well, together with her husband tending their impressive garden, waving to her neighbours, cycling to the village shops.

They would be happy dreams. It is time to leave her alone to enjoy them.

Emma sits alone in her room, the contents of her mind a mixture of misery and confusion. Meeting a real person from her past could have provided her with most of the missing pieces in her life. But she has so many holes in her memory she doesn't know which one to fill first. If only she'd been prepared for the encounter, she could have asked all the questions in an orderly fashion, unlike the improvised grilling she subjected that poor woman to. Mrs Weekes could be the only person in this hospital who genuinely knows her, the only one she can trust. But the poor woman is in hospital for a reason, and she was undoubtedly tired after their conversation. Next time Emma must keep her visit short and ask only a few questions. For now, she considers what she has been able to find out.

Rosa is dead, not shut up in some other part of the hospital unaware of her surroundings. She will never see her best friend again. The full effect of this bombshell will hit her soon enough but there are sure to be more shocks to face. But could there be more positive news, too? From what Mrs Weekes said, her mother is hopefully still alive. Maybe her father is, too. The mere possibility gives Emma a shred of hope to cling to, a reason not to curl up in a ball and roll away into a dark cave in her mind. Whether she likes it or not, she is beginning to learn about this parallel world where she has found herself.

But each ambiguous answer raises even more questions. How did Rosa die? Was it a car accident? Something tells her it wasn't from natural causes. And when did it happen? Months, years, decades ago? But it couldn't have been that long ago because Mrs Weekes said it was the last time she saw her parents. Most mystifying of all, why didn't she go to Rosa's funeral? Mrs Weekes alluded to some hospital stay, yet another piece of her past Emma remembers nothing of. But regardless of this, she and Rosa were best friends. How could she possibly forget such a significant event?

Something is nagging in the quagmire of her mind. Emma has a feeling that she and Rosa argued. It is an instinct rather than a memory, but it is definitely there simmering beneath the surface of her consciousness. And these are only the questions concerning Rosa. But there are more.

What about her own parents? Where are they? If her mother and father are still alive, as she dearly hopes they are, why hasn't one or both visited her in hospital? Yes, there are so many questions that remain unanswered. So much mystery. Once again, she considers the possibility that Mrs Weekes is either wrong or mistaking her for someone else. After all, she did call her Emily first. It is a comforting thought, one that she could quite easily allow herself to linger in even if just for a while.

The drama of the last hour overwhelms her, and she leans her head against the armchair wing. There is nothing else for it. Emma must go back to Mrs Weekes and fill in the grim details. If only she wasn't so tired. She closes her eyes.

CHAPTER SIX

The chipped blue tiles are grouted with hardened brown grease. Twisted beer cans, half-empty wine bottles and thousands of crumbs clutter the worktops. Around her, the combined smell of bacon fat and stale cigarette smoke dominates the air. She wishes Rosa's mother would open the window but is too terrified to ask. With bruised hands, the woman slams two tea plates onto the small table before turning to the pile of dirty dishes on the draining board. Peeling back the white bread, Emma grimaces at the grey, brown paste smeared onto each slice. She hates fish. It makes her breath smell. She watches as Rosa nibbles at the crust of one sandwich half. Rosa is thin, too thin, and it is rare to see food passing between her bow-shaped lips. A man's voice roars in the background and the woman is no longer there. Then a cacophony of screaming, bawling and crashing causes the thin walls to shake. Emma smiles but Rosa's eyes remain on her sandwich. Emma knows she is crying inside so she reaches across the table and touches her arm. Rosa looks up and smiles back. Then she vanishes and Emma is sitting alone.

***

'Mrs Sims?'

It takes only a few seconds for the initial rush of blood to her cheeks to drain away nevertheless she knows he's noticed. She recognises the voice but the face, previously a blur, is now crystal clear. The person near her bed is about twenty- six, tall, slim with light blond hair and he is staring at her with intent. She gazes at the man resembling her favourite half of Starsky and Hutch standing just a few feet away from her. In contrast he, clearly sees only a middle-aged woman in frumpy nightwear facing him. She composes herself. 'Yes. You came before, didn't you?'

'Yes, and I must say you are looking much better,' he says, with a smile. 'Could we have a quick chat?' He knows how to use his good looks to his advantage. Few women would happily refuse such an offer.

But Emma isn't taken in for one minute. His previous visit proved unsuccessful so now he is trying the good cop approach. That's if he really is a detective. Ignoring the banter, she says, 'I'm afraid the doctors are not allowing me to have visitors at the moment. Could you please come back when one of them is here?'

'This won't take long,' he says, looking around the room. 'Only a few questions.'

Just at that moment a student nurse pops her head around the door and says, 'Aww! It's good to see another face in this room. Why don't you fetch a chair in from outside?' she says to the detective.

'Oh, I'm more than happy to stand, nurse. Thank you all the same.' He raises both his thumb and eyebrows.

'If you're sure. I'll be back in a while.' She winks at Emma before closing the door.

Turning back to Emma, the detective smiles displaying a set of perfect white teeth. 'How long have you been in hospital now, Mrs Sims? It must be coming up to a week if I counted correctly on my fingers.'

Emma's skin prickles. For some reason, her instinct is to avoid having anything to do with the policeman regardless of his good looks and apparent charm. 'What is the reason for you visiting again so soon, detective? I'm still not fully recovered.'

'I'll be as gentle as possible.' His expression remains pleasant even as his questions take on a more interrogative tone. 'Have you remembered anymore about the boathouse, Mrs Sims?'

Anymore. How can she convince him that her memory of the boathouse amounts to zero, zilch, zip? The answer to this is she probably can't. 'I am trying, detective, but nothing so far. It's just one of thousands of things I've forgotten. Sorry.'

'Don't apologise, Mrs Sims. I know this is difficult for you. No memory of being in the water?'

'The water?' She screws up her face. 'What do you mean by water?'

'I'm sorry. I should be more specific. I mean the sea. You were in the sea for quite a while, Mrs Sims.'

The sea, the stars, and the waves. Yes, she remembers all that and it makes her shiver.

Observing her facial movements, Carr pushes on further. 'You do remember being in the sea, don't you?'

There seems no reason to deny it, so she nods. After all she's already mentioned it to Mandy, whoever she was.

'How did you end up in the sea?' he continues.

'I think I must have stumbled off the cliff edge somehow, but I don't remember.'

'But there are no cliffs where you were, Mrs Sims.'

'What do you mean, no cliffs? Of course, there are cliffs.'

'Near the boathouse? It's just promenades and walkways.'

He's still talking about the boathouse. She wants to climb back into bed and hide under the sheets. Instead, she shrugs her shoulders. 'Sorry, I was confused. Yes, I remember something about being in the water, but it's very hazy.'

He watches her with his deep blue eyes. 'Never mind. I'm sure it'll come.' After chewing his pen for a few moments he gives a nod, apparently to himself, before continuing. 'I wonder if you could help me out with something that's possibly related to all this. Is it correct that you experienced a severe episode of amnesia several years ago, Mrs Sims?'

They lock eyes. Emma wants to jump through his and swim into a different dream. But it is only her head that is swimming, and she needs to rest it on the wing of the chair. For a few moments, she closes her eyes to block out his presence. But she can't close her ears.

'Mrs Sims. Do you need me to repeat the question?' His voice is a touch sharper.

'No. I heard what you said but I can't help you right now.'

'Why is that?'

She opens her eyes and stares at him. 'Because I can't remember what I did last week let alone several years ago.'

The young detective's expression remains blank for a few seconds before he glances down at his notebook. 'I'm sure there are several explanations for these occurrences even given their coincidental nature.'

Emma rolls her eyes back. 'Can you not talk in riddles? What on earth do you mean by coincidental?'

'Well, let's see.' He turns a page of his notebook over. 'There have only been two instances of amnesia as far as I'm aware, and both came immediately after a serious incident.'

'And I have no idea about either of them. Perhaps it's a weakness in my brain,' she says, not caring how sarcastic this sounds.

The man raises his eyebrows again. 'Obviously, I'm not a doctor but a thirty-year gap in between would be an unusual condition.'

Thirty years! At first, she wants to laugh out loud but quickly remembers she is no longer a young woman. A quick mental calculation sends her mind into overdrive. 'But that would make me ... '

'Twenty-three. The same age as the victim.'

'Victim? Who was it?' Her own question breaks out of her mouth before she has a chance to prepare for the answer.

'A friend of yours. You may not remember her either as you came down with amnesia at the time of being charged with her murder.'

Charged. Murder. It is a killer blow that would have floored Emma if she wasn't already seated. Her head sways and she wishes she could vanish into thin air, just like so much of her life has. So this is what Mrs Weekes was referring to. No wonder the woman didn't want to give any more details when she had a murderer sitting next to her bed. No, wait. This is all crazy. She has never hurt as much as a fly in her whole life, however long that is. And he said she was charged so is he also saying she went to prison?

It is too much to bear. Where is that man? Why isn't he protecting her from these brutal missiles? Right now she would give anything to see him enter the room and march this torturer out through the door like he did before. The sound of a gentle cough piles on the pressure. 'I'm sorry, detective. It was a long time ago. Too long.'

'You've forgotten?' he says, with a smile. Or is it a smirk? 'Well, don't worry. I've got some of the details right here?' He thumbs through his notebook.

'If you already know the answers, why are you asking me?' Emma says, now surprised at her own tone. She should be a quivering wreck but the whole situation is too unreal.

Carr merely shakes his head as if to say, that is not how this works. 'I apologise for any upset this is causing but you will need to talk about this eventually. And,' he turns to look directly into Emma's eyes, 'I honestly believe it will benefit you greatly.'

There is no escape. She braces herself for the oncoming emotional pain. 'Whatever you say.'

The detective produces a second notebook which he quickly thumbs through. 'Your friend's name was Rosa Jones. Is that correct?'

Rosa Jones. Hearing her friend's full name spoken in such an impersonal, matter-of-fact way, Emma feels numb. Rosa is still so present in her dreams - young, vibrant and alive.

'Mrs Sims?' Another cough.

'What happened? What happened to Rosa?'

Detective Carr answers as if he were reading an affidavit in court:

> In the early hours of the morning of the 28th of July 1993, some tourists spotted two women in the water roughly one hundred yards out from the coast at Pickford Bay. The coastguard was alerted, and the women were pulled out. One, Emma Watt, was taken to hospital. The second, Rosa Jones, was declared dead at the scene.

How can you be so cruel? Emma wants to shout out, but she knows it wouldn't change a thing – however they have been said, his words confirm that Rosa has gone. But calling Emma a murderer is as crazy as anything she's been through these past few days. She has to wake up and fight this current battle.

'Wait! If we were both in the water, we probably went for a midnight swim. And we wouldn't have done that unless we were drunk so it was probably an accident. Why was I charged with her murder? It doesn't make sense. I could hardly have dragged her out into the sea, could I?'

'Nobody suggested that you did, Mrs Sims. The beach isn't the only way you could have ended up where you did. And several people stated that a Daniel Merriman was concerned about your whereabouts for roughly one hour before the sighting.

Daniel Merriman. How could she have forgotten her fiancé's name? 'Dan.'

'Yes, Mr Merriman was reported to have been frantic at your unexplained absence from the party for such a long period of time.'

'Where is he?'

'If you would allow me, Mrs Sims.' The detective continues:

The cause of Rosa Jones' death was drowning. However, several cuts were found on her hands. These cuts were thought to be defence wounds. The aforementioned fishermen claimed to have witnessed two people at the cliff edge approximately twenty minutes before coming across Emma Watt and Rosa Jones in the sea. When Emma Watt was questioned about the circumstances leading up to the incident, she claimed not to remember how she ended up in the water. However, a witness saw Emma Watt following Rosa Jones up the cliff path. Emma Watt was carrying an object which resembled the shape of a large kitchen knife. She was charged with Rosa Jones' murder.

His words drift over Emma like a haze of white smoke in a nightclub, disorienting and slightly numbing. The only thing she clasps onto is her own name – Emma Watt. Watt. She's been struggling to remember her surname. It is so reassuring to hear it spoken regardless of the crazy context. But the words keep on coming:

Jonathan Watt was charged with perverting the course of justice. The charges against Emma Watt were later dropped due to a lack of forensic evidence. Up to this day, the exact circumstances leading up to Rosa Jones' death have not been identified.

Jonathan Watt. 'Is my father okay? What happened to him?'

'Your father admitted providing you with an alibi which turned out to be false. He was given a suspended sentence and was lucky not to serve time in prison.'

'But he's a respected composer. His music is performed in concerts around the country.'

'Not after that, he wasn't. His music was shunned after sentencing.'

Her heart is shattered. Somehow she knows her father loves his music, at least as much as he loves his family. And he is brilliant at it. She can remember that he was hoping to write the score

for a Hollywood film which would have pole-vaulted him into
international fame. He risked it all to give her a false alibi. He threw
everything away for her. 'Poor Dad.'

'And Rosa?' There is an accusatory tone to Detective Carr's
query.

'What? Yes, of course. I'm sorry but it hurts when I hear her
name, and it's so hard to know I'll never see her again. We were
very close, you see.'

'Is that so?' Carr says, under his breath.

'Yes, we were. I thought you said you had all the details, detective.'

'Some of the details,' he says, waving his second notebook in the
air. 'This little thing only has room for the brutal facts.'

'Facts? Are you implying that what I said about being close to
Rosa is untrue?'

He raises his hand. 'No, of course not. By facts, I mean names,
dates, places, cause of death, etc.'

Emma wonders how many addresses are in that little notebook,
besides her own of course. Her parents, Mrs Weekes, Dan's. She
could ask the policeman where Dan is. But no. She wants to cherish
her new memory for a while longer. 'I don't know what other
names and places I can tell you. All I can give you is an opinion,
my own opinion.'

'Okay, Mrs Sims. In your opinion, who was responsible for your
friend Rosa Jones's death?'

Emma freezes unable to understand the policeman's meaning.
She needs to dissect the question like it's been spoken in French

or Spanish. *Who was responsible?* Is this something he expects her to know or even have an opinion about? The most likely scenario was that Rosa somehow persuaded her to go out for a midnight swim in the sea and they both got into trouble. How could she be accused of murder for something that hundreds of young people have done? It's ridiculous.

But the detective said something about cuts and a knife. Emma was seen carrying a knife by someone. Did she force Rosa off a cliff and then dive in after her to finish the job? To do such a thing would require a level of callousness that's beyond any normal human being. Surely that's not the person she is. At least she wasn't actually tried *due to lack of forensic evidence* even though she's not sure what that means. Was it just a matter of bored policemen trying to turn a tragic accident into a murder trial just to liven up their dreary jobs? But the image of a knife won't go away. Is it a memory?

'What was the other one?' she asks.

'Other what?' he replies, this time the one confused.

'Earlier you mentioned two serious incidents at the time of my bouts of amnesia. One was Rosa's death. What was the second one?'

'Ah yes, the young woman who visited the boathouse the night you were found in the sea and then went missing.'

'But you said it was a serious incident. Maybe your young woman just went home or has gone on holiday or just doesn't want to speak to you. I can quite understand why.'

'I'm afraid all of those have been ruled out. You see, a boat was found this morning with her body inside.'

'Body?'

'Yes. It was distressing for everyone involved. She'd been dead for several days.'

Emma feels sick. 'Well, that's really horrible but why are you telling me all of this? She must have got lost or killed herself, that's all. What's it got to do with me?'

'You were the person she intended speaking to the night she disappeared. That's why you are being asked about the boathouse.'

'Look, I don't know anything, but even if she came to see me at this boathouse, she was obviously alive when she left if you found her in some boat.'

'Yes, she was certainly alive when she left.' Stepping towards her, the detective pulled something from his inside jacket pocket. 'But it seems she didn't leave by herself.' He hands her a sheet of paper.

Emma squints at the blurry image printed on a white background until the dark smudges morph into recognisable shapes – what looks like a woman being helped onto a boat by another woman. It is night time and one face is still too blurry to distinguish but the other, turned to the side, is a little clearer. It looks like her own profile.

'It was taken by a security camera at eleven pm, roughly an hour after you were last seen at the boathouse. At this point, we cannot confirm the identity of either figure however we are going with the assumption that the one already on the boat is the deceased. From what it is possible to make out, the second bears a resemblance to you.'

'What? How can you say that when half the face is hidden?' She is surprised at the level of her own defensiveness.

Carr shrugs his shoulders. 'That's a good point, and I would hate for a case to rely on incorrect evidence. But the good news is that we have the technology to compare the image to different ones to see if they match up. If one of those figures on the boat is you, Mrs Sims, you should answer this question now rather than later.' He pauses as if for effect and the fear builds up Emma as she locks eyes with the young detective. Finally, he asks the question.

'Did you kill her?'

She watches him, his pen poised ready for an answer she cannot give. It feels like seconds are turning into minutes. Her eyes are heavy, and the room is beginning to spin. He is spinning too but is still waiting for her to speak. Finally, gathering her wits, she decides to confront him, ask him straight out if he is going to arrest her for the murder of someone she has never met. She closes her eyes while formulating the words she will use but the only coherent phrase that comes to mind is *leave me alone.* Without opening her eyes, she says the words and waits for his response. There is no answer. She opens her eyes to an empty room.

Every shade of uniform comes and goes throughout the rest of the day, but Emma can barely acknowledge their presence. Her mind is far away, fled to the sanctuary of her deepest consciousness. It's a kinder place which soothes her shredded soul. Everyone she loves is there and they are alive and well. Her mother and father are smiling at each other just like when she was a child and they were still in love. Dan is there too laughing with her father while avoiding her mother's slightly annoyed expression. She has never been happy with her husband and future son-in-law spending so much time together on their golfing weekends. But that's okay. Emma can cope with such trivial family squabbles. After all, she and Dan are due to be married when they can agree on the date. He wants it sooner than her. But she does love him, and he knows that. She loves everyone there as they are all precious in her life. The only one missing is Rosa who is not welcome in her calm, albeit imaginary space. Yes, this time Emma is well aware that it is not a memory but a creation of her own longing. So, it is up to her who is part of it. And she cannot deal with Rosa being there right now.

CHAPTER SEVEN

Screams of delight emanate from the group of teenagers splashing around in the shimmering river. Boys in their final hurrahs of childhood, enjoying the last of life's carefree days and pretending not to notice the two teenage girls sitting on the bank. The sun is high and strong, and she can feel the heat radiating through the memories. The two friends remove their unflattering school socks, and four slim legs stretch out. Rosa rolls onto her flat stomach and props herself up with her elbows. Then a cloud of smoke rises from behind the wild red curls and a pale arm reaches out towards Emma who takes a drag but then coughs until she cries. Rosa laughs out loud before retrieving the cigarette. Circles of smoke continue to rise up before disappearing across the water while the boys continue to splash around laughing and teasing each other. They get more and more boisterous as they try to outdo one another. One boy stops and turns his head towards the girls. He smiles. The girls are now soaking, and Rosa screams at this boy who is no longer smiling but looks angry, his eyes reflecting the cold river. It is Dan.

***

Emma wakes up in a mixed state of confusion and fear. Being confused has, of course, become all too familiar to her since that dreadful moment she first woke up as a stranger to herself. This morning, however, something is different. After the usual haze dissipates, a more sobering feeling of dread runs through her body as she recalls the previous day's unsettling encounter with the mysterious Detective Carr. What started as a charm offensive by an attractive young man turned into a torrent of ferocious accusations and insinuations. The deaths of two women thirty years apart are the stuff of murder movies, not real life. It is difficult to know which one she should be the most worried about as she has no memory of either.

Tired due to a fitful night's sleep, Emma can barely see beyond the foot of her bed, another affliction she has encountered regularly since waking up. She rubs her eyes in an attempt to banish the floaters which are causing dark and blurry images to dance around the room. Could Detective Carr have been nothing more than a trick of the eye? Anything is possible in this crazy new world. Yet he was definitely there the first time because other people spoke to him – that man and the nurse. But she couldn't see him clearly then so perhaps she carried his voice and name into her imagination.

It's a comforting theory and she decides to stick with it, at least until it's debunked.

A now familiar rattling noise precedes the arrival of someone who Emma is confident is as real as she is. She is pleased to see the top of Tina's face poking out above the steaming water urn and piles of cups.

'You seem really happy in your job, Tina. I envy you.' Emma isn't being untruthful. She would happily switch places with the tea girl.

Tina smiles. 'If I thought I'd be pushing this trolley forever, I'd be crying my eyes out. But I suppose it suits me right now.'

Emma studies the young woman standing in front of her, and for the first time sees past the wishy-washy green uniform. Tina's black hair, dark eyes and red lips are the perfect contrast to her creamy skin, giving her an almost cartoon quality, a Disney princess waiting to be rescued by her Prince Charming. Yes, Emma is feeling very envious at this moment. 'Do you have a boyfriend, Tina?'

The question comes out of nowhere and immediately Emma wants to retract it remembering how irritated she always got when older people pried into her private life as if given the right by their seniority of age. However, Tina shows no such indignation. On the contrary, plonking herself down on Emma's bed, she opens her mouth and a torrent of emotion flows out.

'He wants to get married but I don't feel ready,' she blubbers, her dark eyes drowning in a pool of tears. Without asking, she pulls a tissue from the box on the metal cabinet and blows her nose. 'Look at the state of me. I bet you don't envy me now.'

Emma is shocked to witness Tina's mood transform from care-free to overburdened with problems, her sparkling demeanour reduced to flat hopelessness. Nothing is as it seems. But at least it is a distraction from her own misery. 'Have you told him how you feel? I'm sure he'd understand.'

Tina shakes her head. 'I can't because I don't know how I feel myself. Am I just waiting for someone better to come along or until I'm too old for that to happen?'

'What do you mean by someone better?'

A shameful expression spreads across Tina's perfect features. 'He's good-looking, kind, funny but, and this is going to make me sound so awful, he doesn't earn much and probably never will. At first, I thought it didn't matter, that love was more important than anything, but ...'

'But what, Tina?'

'But my friends go on holidays and have nice clothes and meals and all that. It makes me wonder if I am ready to settle for less.'

'And you would be ready if you really did love him, Tina.' Emma cannot believe she is saying this to a woman she hardly knows. 'Maybe he isn't the right one for you.'

Wiping the tears from her eyes, Tina sits up straight. 'But I do love him, that's the thing. It just frustrates me that he has no ambition beyond a nine-to-five job and football on a Saturday afternoon.'

'Then there's only one thing to do – talk to him.'

'Oh I couldn't possibly. What would he think of me?'

Hearing this brings an ironic smile to Emma's face. In some ways she could be listening to herself but in others, the complete opposite. 'Not being able to open up to each other is hardly the greatest of starts to a lifetime together. Honesty is everything in a relationship.' She sounds like her mother, and she grimaces.

'Can you talk to your husband?' the young woman asks, wiping her now pink cheeks.

Emma needs to bite her tongue to stop herself saying, *your guess is as good as mine*. Instead, she focuses on the relationship she knows plenty about. 'Your boyfriend sounds very much like I used to be, happy to drift along day to day with no desire to achieve anything beyond an easy life. Dan, a man I was once engaged to, was the other extreme. Since being reminded of his name, she wants to keep repeating it in case she forgets it again. Dan was handsome, clever, and ambitious. But he didn't mind the way I was at all as it gave him a reason to organise my life. That sounds a bit too negative actually. I suppose it shows that he loved me for who I was, not who I could or should have been.'

'Any regrets about how things turned out?' Tina asks, before quickly reprimanding herself. 'I'm sorry. That's really not my business.'

There is no way Emma can answer the question honestly because she doesn't even know herself. Instead, she finds herself reminiscing out loud. 'We dated from the end of high school,' she says, her tone warm as she recalls happier times. 'He was such a catch people thought he only went out with me because my father was a successful musician. My friend said Dan clung to my dad like a May bug seeks a bright light. But I think she was being mean. They were close, you see, Dan and my father. Golfing partners.' Her mind drifts away.

One of the most annoying aspects of her relationship with Dan did not actually have anything to do with how they were with each other. Rather it was Dan's relationship with her father. Despite the age gap, her father was the nearest thing to a friend Dan had. The two men shared a love of golf spending several days per month together at the local club. Both Emma and her mother were mystified as to why a young man would enjoy such a middle-aged game. It must be a man thing, they assumed. This was about the only thing she and her mother agreed on; golf was a stupid activity for men who should know better. However, there was more than its pointlessness that was so annoying to Emma. Dan and her father had become regular partners in any amateur competitions they were allowed to enter. There was one weekend when Emma won cinema tickets for the last showing of Pulp Fiction, a film she and Dan had wanted to see for ages but had never got the opportunity. However, it was the same weekend as some ten a penny contest at the local golf course. She argued that it was a game for individuals and that her father could do just as well with any partner as it wouldn't affect his own performance. Yet Dan said the two men had a bond that could not be replicated. We know each other's thoughts, and nobody could replace me, he'd told her in all seriousness. She'd heard her father use a variation of the same nonsense several times. But she loved her father and didn't want to take away any rare moment of pleasure he had.

'Are you okay?'

Emma realises her cheeks are wet and she wipes away the tears that have fallen. 'I'm sorry, Tina. The conversation is supposed to be about you, not me. Tell me more about your boyfriend.'

'Oh, never mind about him. It helps me to hear from women like you. You know what marriage is like and whether you feel the decisions you made were the right ones. I can only guess what to do.'

'Don't let him go, not unless you're absolutely sure.'

'Is that what happened to Dan ... you let him go?' Tina's voice is surprisingly soft.

'I suppose I did.'

'Did you love him?'

Emma pauses before answering. 'I thought I did but now ... he seems so far away. It makes me sad to think about him.'

'Have you seen him much since you split up? I mean is he married too?'

That hurts. 'He could be married but I suppose I wouldn't know. You see, I have no idea where he lives these days, unless he's still in ...,' she stops herself disappearing into her thoughts again. 'It would be good to see him again.'

'You could try and find him; I mean if you wanted to see how he was doing.'

'But how? I wouldn't know where to start and he could be anywhere in the world.'

'You start with the Internet of course.'

'The *what*?'

'The Internet. Haven't you heard of it? There's so much you can find out.'

Emma has no idea what Tina is talking about and assumes it is some new-fangled invention of the past thirty years. But her mind is a whirlpool. 'Could you help me?'

Tina's face lights up. 'Of course, I will. I'm a nosy beggar. Give me as many details as you can, and I'll check the computer after work.'

The computer. That makes sense, Emma thinks. It was only a matter of time before they became more than unreliable word processors. 'What would you be able to find on this Internet, Tina?' she asks, not caring that the question makes her sound even older than fifty-something.

'Oh well, anything that's happened in the world in the past few minutes. Sometimes, I can't believe it myself and it's been around practically all my life.'

Calculating the year of its invention is beyond Emma's frayed mind but she is sure the internet was not around when she was twenty-three. Or even if it was, not even Dan mentioned it. 'What's so wonderful about it?'

'It can tell you whatever you want to know.'

Emma is still none the wiser. 'What is the most amazing thing you could find out?'

For a while, Tina seems lost for words. At last, she says, 'Just about anything that you would find in a book or magazine is on there. And you can translate them into any language you want.'.

'But how can that help you find out where Dan is?' Emma asks.

'It depends on how much information I'm given: which school he went to; what he does for a living. Anything you could give me would help.'

'Well, he's a solicitor and should have his own practice by now. He was just about to get a huge promotion before ... '

'So, he might be a high court judge in The Old Bailey,' Tina says.

But Emma does not laugh. 'I wouldn't be at all surprised as he is ... was so ambitious. But even so, knowing his occupation wouldn't help me find him, would it?'

At this point Tina grimaces. 'Er, well there are other things you can discover ... if you know how.' She lowers her voice and winks. 'And between you and me, I'm a bit of a computer whizz. My brother is even better. He can find anything top secret.'

'That sounds a bit dodgy,' Emma says playfully. If Tina is alluding to something illegal or unethical, it is the last thing Emma is going to worry about.

'Okay. His name's Daniel Merryman.'

Staff Nurse Paul Mason looks surprised when Emma asks him if there are any computers in the hospital. 'Of course. All our medical records are kept this way. And our appointment system has been computerised for years and years. Why do you ask?'

That's not what I mean, Emma thinks, remembering computerized records were around even in her youth. But she's already forgotten the word Tina used when talking about this new phenomenon. 'But can you use them for other things like, er, research?'

'Shopping, you mean,' he rolls his eyes. 'If anybody here has time for that, I need a quiet word with them.' He puts down her arm. 'Blood pressure's looking good. Now let's count those heartbeats, young lady.'

Emma winces and then watches the nurse guide her finger into what looks like a miniature hole punch, and they both wait patiently for the tiny contraption to do its work. At last, she continues with her questions. 'Don't you even get a moment during breaks and lunchtimes?'

'Haha! What are those?'

'You could do with some of my free time,' she says. 'I have more than enough to spare.'

He smiles. 'Are you going out of your mind within these four walls? You must have been here a few weeks now.'

How long has she been here? She has no idea. One minute it's days, the next it's weeks. 'Yes, and it seems like decades. But I shouldn't complain, I suppose.'

'Don't worry. We're always complaining here. Perhaps you should do a bit of browsing for a change. I doubt there's a signal in this room, but you could take it down to one of the communal sitting areas.'

There is too much to what Paul has said that Emma doesn't understand, but she feels they are on the right track. 'Are there computers in these communal areas?'

'Not for public use but your family could bring you one in. Why don't you ask them? Or I could give them a ring,' he says, as he walks out of the room his mind seemingly somewhere else now. But he is brought back by Emma's desperate cry.

'No, no. I can manage, thank you.'

Paul comes back in. 'It's okay. I wouldn't do anything unless you asked me to. Look, there's a library on the second floor. It's for staff but if you ask the librarian nicely, she might let you loose on one of her computers for a bit. Don't say I said that, though.' He winks as he walks out the door once again.

The library is almost empty, and she feels guilty walking past the dusty bookshelves as she makes for the computer room. But right now her mind is focussed on one matter only, and the books won't help her in this. She looks down at the scrap of paper holding the password doubtful she will complete the task ahead without calling for help from the kind librarian. At least the qwerty keyboard is familiar even though touch typing seems to have been consigned to history. She glances at the two other people present, presumably medical students, pounding away at the keyboard with only their index fingers but as fast as any super secretary.

It is clear that a computer has become an essential part of everyday life rather than just an expensive gadget. The reason for this indispensability is one of two things she hopes to find out; the other, far more importantly, is whether all those accusations thrown at her have any grain of truth in them. That policeman has practically accused her of murdering two people, her best friend and a total stranger, that's assuming the second incarnation of Detective Carr is actually a real person rather than a nightmarish figment of her imagination. Libraries have provided various forms of old newspapers for far longer than Emma has been alive, so she supposes the computer in front of her holds the latest versions. The name of the mystery young woman was kept from her so Emma decides to leave that case for now in favour of the one that means more to her.

She begins with her parent's names. Jonathan Watt then Jennifer Watt. Then Jennifer Lovell. Nothing comes up even after every permeation she can think of. Her teachers were always adding an 's' to the end of her surname. But still nothing. So much for the superhighway. Then again her mother is unknown and her father, though a successful musician, was always more behind the scenes. He was as far from being a pop star as she was. And given the Hollywood film score never happened, it's probably not such a surprise that no one has bothered immortalising his name in cyberspace. She has no more luck with Dan's name even though he surely heads his own law firm by now. The one hope is that Tina or her little brother can do better, whether illegally or not.

The next name to try is Rosa's, however, the result is also disappointing. More women than she could ever have imagined being named Rosa Jones come onto the screen – except her Rosa Jones. It doesn't help that the names include women from all over the world – south America, China and, most bizarrely of all, one in the Antarctic. There has to be a way of screening the results further, but she doesn't want to ask the people around her because time is running out. She has only been allotted the computer for twenty minutes. Then a thought comes to her. She types her own name, her real name. And there it is:

Emma Watt has been charged with the murder of Rosa Jones, 23. Watt, also 23, is currently a patient at Caxton Hospital where she has been in a critical condition for the past three weeks. There will be no further comment from the police until after the trial.

There is nothing else. Just three damning lines which shake Emma to the core. Just when she thought all the shocks were over and her mind was settling into something resembling sanity, an invisible hand shakes it around again like a snow globe. The visit from Detective Carr really did happen and wasn't a figment of her bruised imagination. The terrible confirmation is here in black and white. Rosa didn't drown accidentally. She was murdered. And Emma was charged with her murder. She wants to scream but it would make no difference because the words would remain on the screen.

Emma Watt has been charged with the murder of Rosa Jones.

And she was in hospital after that happened, too. Emma was no more memory of Rosa's death than she has of her own present-day life. What on earth happened between her and Rosa that night?

The idea that it was a tragic accident no longer rings true. If it ever did. No. Emma wouldn't have been charged with murder after a skinny-dipping mishap. They must have had a row of some sort. But they never quarrelled, even during the later years. They may have had their catty moments, sulky even, but both of them managed to keep a lid on their temper. Perhaps they could have been more open about their feelings. Hurt, anger, jealousy. It doesn't always do to keep things bottled up inside as they might explode when the lid finally comes off. Was that what happened?

And it seems she disappeared from the party if what the detective said about Dan looking for her was true. The detective who must be real. She needs to remember the truth, or she could end up in prison. Again? She may have been locked up once. Perhaps she is still there, and her current existence is one long hallucination. But the newspaper report says charged. Emma clearly wasn't convicted. Or was she? No. It would say, wouldn't it? Newspapers always report the arrests and the trials, but not so much the dropped charges. The innocent are not as newsworthy as the guilty. And the detective said the case remains unsolved so no one else was found guilty? To Emma's muddled mind, there is hardly evidence to discard the swimming misadventure theory. She wonders why the police are re-investigating Rosa's death after such a long time. Or is Detective Carr just a rogue cop with a bee in his bonnet? If so, he obviously thinks she's guilty or he wouldn't be risking his job in this way.

The dreadful possibilities bounce around Emma's head until she can bear it no longer. There must be a mistake, she tells herself. Perhaps the article was the result of a misquote. She spends the rest of her allotted time frantically searching for more articles but to no avail. For a crazy few seconds, she wonders if the name on the screen belongs to a completely different woman. She desperately wants that to be the answer. After all, it would explain so much if she and the real Emma Sims have somehow changed places and are living each other's lives. That would make everything clear as day instead of dark as night.

But this comforting thought only lasts seconds because the name on the screen is Emma Watt, not Emma Sims. The two women are one and the same. The only thing that makes any sense is what she's been told by everyone around her. A few weeks ago, an incident at sea caused her to lose half her life, more than half, along with the joy, the pain, and the horror. It has left her a mere shell of what she must once have been. She has to find those missing years before she loses her life completely.

CHAPTER EIGHT

They are in a bedroom expensively decorated with plush scattered curtains and lavish wall hangings. From a cd player, a familiar REM rift repeats endlessly. Perhaps the cd is scratched but nobody seems to notice, or they don't care. Rosa is hanging out of a Georgian window, buried behind the blush pink velvet curtain, but smoke from her cigarette is still drifting inside. Emma sprays perfume and waves a pillow around the space between Rosa and the locked door. She is worried in case it won't be enough to pass the test of her mother's bloodhound nostrils. Rosa closes the window and switches the cd player off, but the silence does not last long. The jangly guitar music is replaced by various piano chords and arpeggios that are now able to dominate the airwaves. Her father is working hard downstairs. She closes her eyes and pictures him sitting at the grand piano scribbling notes onto endless sheets of paper, crossing them out again, clasping his head in his hands then turning his face to her and smiling. His eyes are melancholy, filled with both love and sadness. It is as if he is really there. She wonders if he can see her too and steps forward to hug him. But he turns away again.

***

A hand touches Emma's shoulder, and she opens her eyes to see a man crouching over her. It takes her a few moments to realise who it is. He looks like a senior doctor, but she knows he isn't.

The man who claims to own her, to be her husband, jolts as if he has suffered an electric shock. 'I'm sorry, Darling. I didn't mean to wake you.' He grabs a plastic chair and sits just a few feet away.

Considering earlier encounters, moving as he has done into her personal space is a bold move. The fact that she hasn't screamed in horror he probably considers a step in the right direction. However, to Emma, he is no longer the person she fears most and having used up all her adrenalin on previous panics, she stays calm and visually examines the man in front of her.

He, Mr Sims, is distinguished looking even discounting the obvious tailormade suit which oozes quality. He looks younger than the first time she saw him. In fact, he looks younger than her. Although speckled with grey, his hair is thick and slightly gelled to grow upwards in a style she's always thought quite attractive. His body is lean with no sign of the middle-aged spread that afflicts so many men and women in the same age group. He is a good-looking man clearly successful in whatever job he does. And he looks more familiar each time she sees him.

'I've had a word with the doctor. He said you were doing well and should be allowed home soon.' His voice is soft and upbeat, but after observing Emma's eyes, he qualifies his words. 'Of course, nothing is going to happen until you feel completely ready, Darling.'

She nods. It is okay. Nobody is going to force her to leave what has become her little sanctuary - the flimsy four walls around her. Only twice has she stepped outside them and both those adventures merely brought bad news. But at some point in the near future, when Mrs Weekes has rested, Emma knows she will have to go back for more. Emma will reassure her that she is ready to cope with any information about Rosa's death, and even her own arrest.

'Thelma sent this for you, Darling. She also sends her apologies for not visiting yet but she has after-school meetings every day what with the inspection looming.'

Darling. Mrs Sims. Emma is not sure which mode of address irks her more. All the same, she does not allow such trivial matters to overcome her. 'Oh, thanks,' she says, taking the gift bag from him and laying it down on the floor.

'Rather than clutter up this room with my own unwanted gifts, I thought it wiser to let you buy your own.' He takes out his wallet and places a bank card on the arm of her chair.

Emma looks at him blank-faced.

'There's a little shop on the ground floor,' he says quickly. 'I see from your expression you haven't been down there yet.'

'A shop?' She looks up at him as if he has said a word she doesn't understand.

He smiles. 'Yes, it's more Co-op than House of Fraser, but there's room enough for browsing and it sells most things. I'm not sure about Malbec though.'

It seems bizarre that anyone would want to go shopping while a patient in hospital, but at least the card now makes sense. There is one problem which she doesn't know how to broach. Instead, she merely stares at the name written on the plastic rectangle. MRS EMMA K SIMS.

It takes a few seconds for the middle initial to mean anything to Emma. K? She is just about to ask the virtual stranger what her middle name is when it suddenly comes to her – Katherine. How much more of herself has she lost? Even the card looks alien. 'I can't use that. I don't know the pin number,' she says, almost to herself.

'Well that's a surprise,' he laughs. 'Then it's just as well I asked our daughter for it.'

Emma's expression remains blank.

'You've let her use it enough times, Darling. Now listen carefully as I will say this only once: Each digit is the birth month of your mother, father and you in that order. What are the chances, eh?'

The stilted conversation is interrupted when Tina pops her head around the door. 'Oh, sorry to disturb you,' she says, looking at Mr Sims. 'I just wanted to see how you were.'

'I'm better now, thanks,' Emma says, wondering if the im-promptu visit is related to news on Dan. She can feel herself getting excited at the thought of being able to contact him and wishes she could reward Tina in some way.

'I might forget the number. Have you got any cash on you?' Her voice is robotic so she can disassociate herself from the question. Asking a strange man for money is excruciating. Even if he is supposed to be her husband, she is not there yet. She doubts she will ever be.

'Sorry, I should have thought of that. There's a cash machine too if you want to have some money here,' he continues. 'Don't get too much out though. You can't trust anyone no matter how helpful they are.'

Silence falls around them and Emma is unnerved. She decides the time has come to find out about the world waiting for her outside. 'Who is at home?'

The man shows no surprise at the question as if it is one he has heard many times before. 'Well, no one at the moment because we are both here.' He looks at his watch. 'Even Martha will have left now. She's not one to hang about.'

'Martha?'

'Don't worry. I told her not to clean your bedroom until you come home. She gave me a look, though, as if I was accusing her of snooping ... or worse.'

Your bedroom. Maybe they aren't married after all. But then she remembers the ring. He is wearing one too which she thinks rather odd. Her father never wore one. 'Are you my only visitor?' She only knows him as Mr Sims, having forgotten the name he used in the panic of their initial meeting.

He looks embarrassed. 'For now. They were only allowing next of kin for the first few weeks. It's more lax now but, as I told you earlier, Thelma is up to her eyes in school meetings. Susanna will be in soon but it's quite a long way for her to travel.'

Next of kin. Stay calm, she tells herself. 'That's okay. Where is this hospital?'

'What do you mean?'

'Where am I right now?'

'Oh, I see. Stanford.'

'Where's that? I don't recognise the name.'

'Well, I think this place may have been called something else before they extended it. Anyway, it's not far from your hometown. This was the closest hospital to the pickup.'

'Pickup?'

'When the helicopter picked you up from the water. It takes a couple of hours to get here so I doubt you'll get many visitors.'

'But you said it is near home.'

'Your childhood home, Emma. *We* live in Pickford.'

Emma has never heard of Pickford either but doesn't bother saying so. It is not the biggest mystery she's encountered lately.

'Why don't we go for a walk, Darling? It'll do you good to get out of this room.'

How many times has he called her *Darling* already? She nods. Why not?

They amble down the same sterile corridor Emma was in a few days ago. Although everything looks similar, nothing is familiar enough and there is no landmark to signpost the room in which she so recently sat talking to Mrs Weekes. What if she'd dreamed the whole thing? This thought sends a violent shudder through her body, so she banishes it to the back of her mind. The mental turmoil adds to her physical weakness, and she stumbles several times. He insists that she links her arm in his, and she hasn't the strength to resist so they continue on their way, this time with him keeping her on course. It isn't so bad. She imagines he is a nurse. So many of the nurses are male after all. Once they reach the end of the corridor unexpected panic sets in and she attempts to turn around, but he keeps moving her forward. It is a battle he is always going to win. Finally, he propels them both through a gap in the wall into a tiny courtyard.

'The air's not exactly fresh,' he says, glancing at the high glass walls around them, 'but it's as close as we'll get to the great outdoors for now.'

Emma sits on a wooden bench, her eyes settling on the only other occupant of the courtyard: a woman of middle age puffing on a cigarette. Circles of smoke swirl around in the air. Somehow the fumes do not carry over but instead vanish into nothing. Emma feels an affinity with the woman in her sad solitude, cut off from the rest of the world just for that moment in time. Whatever she is thinking will stay locked inside the walls of her mind, with no one around to disturb it. But for once Emma isn't alone so she returns to her companion, albeit a virtual stranger.

'Have you eaten?' The question comes out of her lips but not from her mind. It is as if it is second nature to ask, like a question she's asked so many times before. Perhaps she really is his wife.

It also seems second nature for Mr Sims to hear it. 'Not yet. I sent Julia out for a sandwich, but she came back with prawn mayonnaise. Twenty years my secretary and she forgets about my seafood allergy. Unless she's trying to kill me of course.'

His attempt at dark humour brings a slight smile to Emma's face. 'I hate prawns too,' she says as if the man sitting next to her wouldn't know that. The man! For someone who is supposed to be her husband, his first name is still a complete blank. Learning his name might help her realise if she does indeed know him. She thinks of the names she's heard in the past few minutes. *Susanna, Julia, Martha*. But not his. Of course, he wouldn't use his own name in a conversation so how on earth will she discover it? Now an idea comes to her; it will be like playing a little game.

'Does she still call you Mr Sims after all this time?'

'Julia? Only when she's particularly annoyed with me. Other than that, it's Dave, which of course you hate.'

So that is his name. David. It means nothing to her. She needs more. 'Dave doesn't suit you, does it? It's a bit tradesman.' Could he possibly be a builder of some sort? She doubts it.

He laughs. 'Gosh! I didn't know you were such a snob. Wait, of course, I did because you used to look down your nose at me. Well, you still do.' He winks but then his voice drops. 'What's this sudden interest in Julia?'

'Just making conversation, David.'

'Well, could we at least talk about more important people? You, for instance.' He clasps her hand in his. 'Are you still having headaches, Darling?'

She lifts her hand free and brushes her hair back. 'You sound like a doctor.' His dignified demeanour is a match for Dr Syed's.

'A lawyer can ask questions too,' he replies, with a grin.

So, he is a lawyer, just like Dan. Dan. It is a struggle to keep her mind from wandering back to Tina. She wants to ask David about him, but something tells her not to. Since that first horrible encounter, he has shown nothing but concern and kindness towards her. Yet something is missing from his eyes. Is it love? He didn't appear surprised or hurt when she withdrew her hand and, if they really are married, she wonders how close a couple they are. It is as if he is going through the motions. He is acting the dutiful husband, but she wonders what is behind the costume. Reading people is something she's always been able to do. And David is putting on a performance. She doesn't know how he usually acts so how could she possibly know if she loves him? Not the way she loves ... loved Dan.

She closes her eyes to shut David out of her private moment. Dan's face comes back to her, and she lets out an involuntary sigh. She pictures him standing in the doorway of their flat, his suit trousers as crumpled as his fair hair. The sockets of his eyes are dark, and he looks annoyed. She searches her mind for a happier image but without success. How desperate she is to see him again, even if he is old like her.

There is movement from across the courtyard. Emma's mind returns to her current situation, and she wonders how long has passed since she last spoke. They both look across at the other woman who is now walking back towards them, a saline drip dragging along behind her. She doesn't acknowledge them as she passes but this is hospital etiquette: no greetings, no small talk, just private thoughts.

'David, do you remember Rosa?'

David's countenance shifts. He looks shaken, the first glitch in his performance. 'Why are you asking this now?'

'Do you?'

'Er, yes I do.'

'What happened to her?'

The tilt of his head suggests that the question has surprised rather than unnerved him. 'Emma, that was years ago.'

'How did she die?'

'Emma, this isn't the time or the place to drag up the past.'

This time she shouts at him. 'How did she die?'

He jolts in his seat. Now he is unnerved. All he can do is shake his head.

'Why won't you tell me?'

'She drowned.' He shouts the words, and it is as well their audience of one has gone back inside.

Even though it is not the first time she has heard the terrible phrase, Emma cannot find her own words to formulate a response. She merely stares at him.

At last, he seems to regain his composure. 'It was a long time ago, and it wasn't your fault.'

It wasn't your fault. 'What happened?'

'It was the night of your parents' party. Everyone assumed the two of you went for a midnight swim and Rosa got into difficulty. That's as much as anyone knows.'

'Why didn't I go to the funeral?'

'Who told you that? Who have you been talking to about this? Wait! Has that damned detective been back here?'

'Mrs Weekes told me. I was talking to her earlier today. She helped fill in some memory gaps.'

'Mrs Weekes?' he says. 'Who is she? Did she visit you?'

Emma looks at him suspiciously. 'No. She's a patient here, too. Don't you remember her? She lives across the lane.'

He looks confused. 'We don't live near a lane.'

'The lane by my parent's house. Mrs Weekes lives on the other side. Hers is the only other house for miles.'

'Gosh, and she's still alive?'

'Obviously, she's still alive. I wasn't imagining it. Do you remember her?'

'Vaguely. I think she was at the par... well, let's not bring that up now.'

Emma finds herself getting muddled again. She needs to keep herself focussed on one question at a time. 'You haven't told me why I didn't go to Rosa's funeral.'

'You weren't well, that's why. I didn't go either for that matter.'

So, he knew Rosa too but probably not much. Now for the killer question. 'Why was I charged with her murder?'

His face grows paler at each word. He takes out a handkerchief and dabs his bone-dry forehead. 'Why would she talk about that?' he mutters to himself.

'It wasn't Mrs Weekes who told me.'

He turns to her, his handkerchief in mid-air. 'What do you mean? Oh, wait a minute. Trust that to come back to you first.'

'No, I don't remember anything about it. The detective told me. I thought maybe I dreamt it, but you've just confirmed it was real.'

'What detective, Emma?'

'The same one who came before. The one called Carr. He practically accused me of being a con artist as well as a double murderer.'

'*Double* murderer?' His mouth drops open. 'What double murder?'

'Rosa's and a woman who I sailed off with on some pea green boat.'

'What woman, Emma? What boat?'

'The woman who came to the boathouse.' She can't believe she's actually the one using that word. 'Apparently, we disappeared together, and she's turned up dead, decayed and adrift.'

He shakes his head. 'There is no dead woman in a boat. In my line of work, I would have heard about it.'

Emma wonders if that could be right. The detective might have been playing with her mind. 'Well, that's a relief. But what he said about Rosa was true, wasn't it? Now that would be some joke I would gladly laugh about right now.'

But David looks far from amused, his complexion turning from white to full-blooded in nanoseconds. 'How dare he? The charge was an outrage. You were found innocent.'

'But I wasn't found innocent, was I? The charges were dropped through lack of evidence. It's not the same thing at all.'

'It is in my world,' he says angrily. 'What's the point of having a justice system if we don't use it properly? There was no evidence to charge you, Emma.'

'There must have been something,' she argues. 'Maybe I did kill Rosa. The case was only dropped because there was no forensic evidence, whatever that means. I'm sure you know.'

'For goodness' sake! The case was dropped after they found new evidence. You are not a murderer, Emma.'

'What new evidence? And the police must have believed someone killed Rosa, killed my best friend. Yet, you said it was an accident, that we were night swimming. If that really was what we were doing, why should the police think it was murder? And how was I charged and then cleared if there wasn't a trial? None of this makes any sense. What you are telling me makes no sense.'

'It makes no sense to you because you can't remember everything. So, maybe I am omitting some of the more intricate details. It was thirty years ago. I can barely remember them myself.'

Emma is unsure whether David is lying or his memory is as muddled as hers. He hasn't mentioned anything about a knife or Emma having gone missing from her parents' party again. On the other hand, the detective never told her about any new evidence that persuaded them to drop the charge. Her head is spinning.

'So, tell me what you do remember, David. Why was the charge dropped? That's one intricate detail you must remember.' Hearing the sarcasm in her own voice, she tries to calm down. 'David, you said there was no trial. Surely they wouldn't drop a murder investigation just like that.' But her more conciliatory tone has the opposite effect intended.

David digs his heels in further. 'Okay.' He puts away his handkerchief and leans towards her. 'It was thirty years ago, and I've been in the middle of hundreds of criminal cases since that one. We have enough to deal with now without raking over old coals that have long burnt out. You've been doing so well, Emma, but we've still got some way to go. Keep focussed on getting well and the past will right itself soon enough.'

Emma tries to regain control of the conversation by moving it forward. 'David, why can't I remember Rosa dying?' It doesn't work.

'Like I said, you weren't well.' He stands up to signal the end of his part in this particular discussion. 'Come on. Let's go back inside.'

As they walk back down the corridor, Emma glances into each room they pass looking for something that rings a bell. Determined to gain one last insight from the exhausting experience with David Sims, her mind is now focussed on introducing him to her old neighbour. She begins to lose hope, but at last, she notices the yellow bin. 'There's Mrs Weekes' room. Let's go and talk to her. She might remember you.'

'Oh, let's not disturb her now. She might have visitors.'

'Then we'll come back. Quick! I want her to see you.'

In her hurry, she leaves him behind. It is the most enthusiastic she's felt since waking up. Two people from different stages of her life together in the same room. Will their stories match? He says he remembers Mrs Weekes, but does she remember him? Did she ever see Emma and David together as a couple, or just individually? There are so many uncertainties, too many to clarify in another brief meeting. She will need to take things in stages. The first should be David's presence in Emma's younger life. Whatever Mrs Weekes says, Emma will have to accept as true. Despite herself, she shudders.

When she enters the room the elderly woman is sleeping, at least that is what Emma first thinks. But there is something odd about the way she is lying with her knees curled up to her chin. Emma stares at the dying woman. Long buried memories resurface -the last image of her grandmother, her mother's tears, her father's hug. Now Emma is crying for this woman she barely remembers.

Once again there is a hand on her shoulder, this time a female hand, followed by comforting words. 'Don't feel bad. It's never easy.' The nurse gently manoeuvres Emma out of the room.

Emma looks at David, and for a split second, she thinks he looks relieved. Then she recalls his reluctance to face Mrs Weekes. Inside her head, an array of emotions is building up like molten rock. It erupts. 'You killed her,' she screams. 'You killed her so she wouldn't tell me.'

'Mrs Sims, do be quiet. You are acting hysterical.' It is the same nurse who was so sympathetic just seconds before. 'Come on now. Let's take you back.'

Emma feels herself being led back down the corridor and into the reassuring familiarity of her own hospital room. 'Don't let him near me, will you? Please keep him away from me. Call Dan. I want Dan.'

David stands in the doorway. Emma is cowering in her chair. They have come full circle.

CHAPTER NINE

Rosa stands alone on the well-worn stage, fake blood dripping from the pale hand that she holds up in the air. She cries out in sorrowful pain, her red eyes filled with madness and guilt, her pale cheeks wet with tears. A final anguished wail and she is lying on the splintered floorboards. Gradually the lights lower until she disappears from sight. There is silence before some muted applause. Dan peers out from behind the musty red curtain, the gleam in his eyes visible even in the dimness. He is still wearing a crown clearly made of cardboard. His devilish eyes scan the hall and rest on Emma. Her heart jumps and she waves to him. At least she thinks she is waving but her arms are not visible even to her. The curtains fall and there is complete darkness. Then a sliver of light can be seen as the curtain moves again. Dan is no longer visible, so she looks for Rosa. Through a gap in the curtain, she sees her. Rosa is still wearing the white gown which they both stitched together from old bedsheets. Somehow it suits her. An ethereal

image hidden from everyone except Emma. And she knows Rosa
can see her, too.

**

Emma has never been to France or Spain, but now she feels as
if she knows both countries as well as anybody else. While the
glamorous presenter exhibits yet another ramshackle property in
the mountains, Emma wonders how desperate the buyers must
be. Why would anyone want to move to a foreign country where
you couldn't understand any of the neighbours? By the time you
learnt the language and culture, you'd be too old to participate in
community life. You would be watching from the periphery, like
a team reserve who never gets to join the match. A spectator. Yet
the television show is as addictive as it is repetitive, and Emma has
watched one after the other. Besides it takes her mind off her own
discombobulation, a word she's picked up from the programme.
Moreover it helps her forget about David Sims, Detective Carr,
and poor Mrs Weekes, the latest in a growing run of setbacks.

It is telling that of all the many dozens of channels available,
Emma has chosen one that isn't filled with worrying detail. When
the nurse first set up the bedside television, she left Emma watching a news channel, a mystery to its new viewer. Like a scratched
record, the newsreaders said the same thing over and over again,
or at least every fifteen minutes. For Emma, each name was a
new name. The politicians, celebrities, and sports stars were all
unknown to her. If that wasn't unsettling enough, journalists out

on location gave a preview to the life outside of Emma's bubble. And from what she can see, it's better remaining where she is.

There are more cars and bikes on the road, this is certain. The people look different too, more multicultural. All that is fine. The depressing images coming from the run-down high streets shown are not. It had already started back in the eighties and early nineties, of course, shoppers deserting the businesses in favour of the out-of-town conveniences. But now it is so much worse. Even the sky seems greyer. She isn't looking forward to stepping outside the hospital though she knows that moment must come eventually. For the time being, she will enjoy the near fantasy world of the Mediterranean.

On the television screen gondolas and yachts float down a wide canal, its shimmering green water lined with Baroque buildings of numerous pastel shades. This glorious image is replaced by one of her mother sitting outside a café in uptown Venice - a moment in time photographed by a mystery companion. Emma rests her head on the pillow and allows the memories to flow.

How her mother loved Italy. As part of her university studies, she'd spent a year in Rome and was swept away by the high culture, arts and fashion. Despite already dating Emma's father, she planned to return immediately after graduating.

"I wanted to open up a boutique, but life got in the way," she would say, with her usual tactlessness.

Emma knows she wasn't planned, and that her parents were caught out by the treacherous combination of contraceptives and alcohol. The young couple with so many romantic dreams ended up in a grubby rented flat above a London takeaway, and Jennifer never got her boutique. In fact, she never worked at all, settling into the role of housewife for the next eighteen years until Emma left for university herself. But Jennifer Watt was no bird in a gilded cage sitting at home waiting for random attention from her busy working husband. With Emma's father based at home, her mother often enjoyed several solo trips to Italy and France, thriving on the time she had to herself.

Images of Jennifer Watt stepping in and out of a taxi, the driver carrying her travel bags, the kisses on both cheeks. It was a gesture she came across on one of her many continental holidays bringing it home to use on her friends and family. Friends were impressed but the teenage Emma found it plain embarrassing, especially when her mother hugged Emma's friends, too. Much to her annoyance they always loved it. Rosa in particular only ever said wonderful things about Emma's mother.

"She's so stylish, so glamorous. You should be so proud of your mum, Emma. I wish my mother was more like her."

Rosa should wish her mother was more like anyone, Emma thought at the time. Now older, she realises that Mrs Jones did the best she could under difficult circumstances. The only shopping trips she could make on her invalidity benefits were to the discount stores. Her threadbare clothes were cheap, dowdy and unflattering. It was a marked contrast to Emma's own mother who, when not abroad, was on the high street accustoming herself to the latest haute couture. And it was worth the effort. Jennifer Watt was the epitome of understated wealth. The colours of her daywear were always fairly bland like beige and grey; her Gabor shoes were flat and serviceable; her honey-blonde hair swept in a loose bun. The only concession to brightness was the lipstick which was always coral. Emma wonders if she still wears it. She hopes she does.

The next programme is starting, its jolly theme music preventing Emma from descending into tearful nostalgia. This time the location is Spain. She laughs to herself knowing that the unsuspecting property buyers will end up in the hills far away from the very reason they wanted to move to the Costa del Sol in the first place.

'Hiya.'

It is like looking in a mirror except the dark hair is a little messier with split ends begging to be removed. And the shape of the body is the same but slouched as if there were no skeleton to hold it up. It is the body of a woman with little interest in her appearance. The only evidence of muscle usage is that the large book held under one arm does not fall to the floor. Nothing needs to be said. Emma already knows what is coming. In the crazy parallel universe she finds herself in, the nervous-looking young woman is clearly meant to be her daughter.

'I'm glad you managed to work out the television. Ooh, I could envy you watching property programmes all day,' the young woman says, with a smile that does not reach her eyes.

Emma doesn't answer wishing instead she could carry on watching the property programme rather than face this next challenge.

Clearly, her visitor hasn't noticed as she continues talking, 'I'm sorry I couldn't get here till now. There's no direct bus on a train and you know I hate motorway driving.'

That doesn't sound like a good enough excuse to Emma, and she feels it gives her the excuse to delay her response further.

'How are you feeling, Mum? To be honest I thought you'd be sleeping.' The woman obviously knows about the mild sedation Emma was given after her latest bout of hysteria.

Emma continues to examine the stranger's appearance, this time her dress sense. She isn't wearing any makeup. Her hair doesn't look brushed. And those tight jeans are so out of date. Emma used to wear ones just like them when she was in college. But that was in the eighties. For one horrible moment, she wonders if they are actually her jeans. But that would be ridiculous, she tells herself.

'I've been thinking about the boathouse. I can't believe you went off by yourself, especially after drinking. You're supposed to be the sensible one, Mum.'

The boathouse reference again. Emma makes a mental note that she should start writing the references down before she forgets them all. But she knows she will probably forget the mental ones, too. If only she had one of those notebooks.

'Are you okay? Did you hear what I said?'

As much as she wants to, Emma supposes that she can't go on ignoring her visitor. The concern in the other woman's voice forces her to fake a smile despite her sinking mood. The idea of being a mother to a woman older than her, or rather the age she still feels she really is, doesn't bother her a great deal. At least she can relate to the young woman. It isn't as disturbing as the thought of being married to David, a man older than her own father ... her father.

'I can't stay long because I've left Chloe with a friend.' She slumps rather than sits in the visitor's chair.

'Which friend?' Her own question surprises Emma considering she feels no connection to these latest people in her new life.

'Carrie. I don't think you've met her. Remember that wedding ... oh never mind.'

Emma doesn't know what to say having no interest in Chloe or Carrie, or even her own 'daughter', so she thinks about saying nothing. However, the silence is deafening, and she knows it is her turn to speak. But to say what? Deciding on a suitable topic of conversation is not easy. Certain words spin around in her head: David; detective; drowning. She chooses the one that means far more to her and has climbed to the top of her jumbled thoughts.

'Do you know where Dan is?' Since the name has re- embedded itself in her brain, all she wants to do is scream it out loud. As it is, she merely mumbles it.

'What did you say?' There is a hint of disappointment in the young woman's tone.

Emma speaks louder this time. 'Do you know where Dan is?'

'Who is Dan, Mum? I don't think I've heard that name before. Is he one of Dad's friends?'

Keeping her emotions in check, Emma replies, 'No, don't worry about it. It's nice to see you. Thanks for coming.' The words are ridiculously formal, so she smiles once again.

Reading the smile as a green light, the young woman stands up and moves closer to Emma. 'Mum, why did you do it? Are you so unhappy with Dad? I thought you too were getting on better.' Her voice is trembling.

Emma doesn't know which of the latest episodes "it" refers to. Is it the clumsy suicide attempt after her first meeting with David or the hysterical display outside Mrs Weekes' room? Not to mention whatever happened at the boathouse. One thing that is certain is the pain in the other woman's voice. It is the pain of a family member. This is undeniable. If the young woman is putting on an act, it is a performance that deserves an Oscar. Emma decides to play her role in the surreal scene. Her lines include an element of truth.

'I'm sorry. Since I woke up, I've been scared and confused because I don't know why I'm in hospital. The fall must have bashed my senses around.' She is convincing herself as much as anyone. 'Although my mind is still all over the place, the sense of panic and fear is becoming less and less all the time. I'm sure I'll be back to normal soon.'

'Of course, you will be, Mum. Look, about that night, there is something I need to ask you. Why did that woman want to speak to you?'

Emma stares at the other woman. In only a few minutes, 'her daughter' has asked her about the boathouse and the young woman who supposedly turned up unexpectedly. It is as though she and the detective are working together. This fact persuades Emma to tread carefully. 'To be quite honest I don't remember meeting her. I wish I did because it would make things a little clearer.'

'But we all saw you leaving the boathouse so you must remember meeting her, Mum.'

No, I don't, Emma thinks. 'Then I suppose I must have. Who saw us together?'

The woman looks confused. 'You were in the courtyard talking to her when Dad looked over. Didn't he tell you?'

Emma shakes her head. 'Maybe he did. I must have forgotten. Like I said my mind is a mess at the moment.'

'But that's because of the accident. I'm talking about before that happened. There must have been a reason for you to be talking to the woman in the first place. And now she's dead.'

And now she's dead. So that's why she keeps asking me about that woman? Is she accusing her too? Emma wonders if David was lying to her when he insisted there was no dead woman in a boat. It is too much for her to think about right now. 'That's terrible but I'm sure I don't know her even if we did meet briefly.'

'Okay. How did you end up in the sea miles away from the boathouse?'

It's a crazy scenario and Emma cannot scramble any defensive response. She wants to joke about a pea-green boat again but knows it is no laughing matter. Instead, she shakes her head and speaks the truth. 'Perhaps I was lost. Perhaps I was looking for everyone else.'

The young woman's expression reflects the sadness of what is said, and for a second her face takes on the identical image of

Emma's twenty-three-year-old self as if she had lost her own identity. 'You make it sound as though we weren't there.'

Her words make Emma think about what is real. She reaches out and touches the young woman to make sure she is matter and not merely a hologram or figment of Emma's imagination. Again the woman misreads the action. Laying her head on Emma's stomach she begins to cry. Yes, her tears are undeniably real.

'Hey don't cry. I'm okay.' It is an awkward moment of intimacy that Emma desperately wants to withdraw from. She chooses to do so by changing the subject slightly. 'Have you heard any more about my treatment?'

The mood of the young woman whose name is still a mystery seems to improve as a result of Emma's question. She straightens up and clasps her hands as if in prayer. 'Dad is popping in later once he's met with the doctor. I think they are going to do some tests, and if all is well you'll be allowed home soon after.'

Emma suppresses the hysteria rising inside her and nods. 'Home! I don't feel ...' She doesn't know how to finish the sentence. Their home, not hers. How is she supposed to adapt to that? First, a wife, then a mother, and finally, a grandmother. Are there any more shocks to be had? If so, she can't imagine anything worse than going 'home' to a strange man.

'The nurse says you're still a bit disoriented from all the drugs; that's putting it mildly, I guess. Then there's the shock of the accident. He said it can take a while for some patients to recover psychologically as well as physically.'

'I think I might need more time for everything to come back to me.'

'Well, Thelma's promised to cook some of her patties as a welcome home meal. No doubt you remember how delicious they are.'

Thelma. She's heard that name before. 'Who's Thelma?'

'Mum, she's your best friend. In fact, she's your only friend,' Susanna says, giving an unconvincing laugh.

Emma shrugs. 'I don't like pasties.'

'Patties, Mum. Jamaican patties. And we all love them. You, especially.'

There is little point in continuing with this particular topic of conversation. 'Never mind. I'm sure it'll all come back to me soon enough.'

For the first time, the young woman pulls out the book that is still under her arm and hands it to Emma. 'These might help.'

It is heavier than a book should be, and Emma looks at it with a sense of dread. Then she realises it is not a book after all. It is a photograph album. Her heart rate slows to match the pace with which she opens the floral cover, but she only needs to view the first page. There is no need to go further.

Staring back at her is David, his hair a bit less white, with one arm around a teenage version of the young woman claiming to be her daughter. With his other arm, he hugs a teenage boy. And there, arm outstretched and head against David is Emma. And she is smiling. It is indisputable. Like mirrors, cameras never lie. She closes the cover and sobs.

The young woman jumps up and places her hand on Emma's. 'The nurse told me that people who've suffered trauma can forget things. It's like the mind protecting them. But you're safe now. Everyone is here for you. We were a happy family once, Mum. We can be again.'

But tears are now running uncontrollably down Emma's face as she realises where the conversation is going. Unable to take part in the pretence any longer, she covers her wet eyes with her healthy arm. 'I don't feel well enough yet. Leave me here ... please.'

'I know it's soon, but they need the bed. If you don't go home in the next couple of weeks, they'll have to ...' The voice has become harder.

'Have to what?' What could be worse?

'Admit you to a mental hospital, Mum. Is that what you want?'

A mental hospital. Is that it? Has she lost her mind? It is something she has not considered, not since waking up so many weeks ago. Not seriously. Paradoxically, it would be a sane and rational explanation for what she is going through. She manages to shrug her shoulders to signal her indecision. An institution should give her time to dwell on her circumstances and remove the pressure to make a decision on her next move. But she would be trapped here, maybe forever.

'Well? Will you see Dad? I know things have been difficult between you two, but he's trying his best.' Her voice has mellowed from its earlier irritable tone.

However, Emma doesn't answer because she is lost in thought, the thought that she is crazy. It doesn't scare her but being locked up in a padded cell does. She needs to get out of here whatever the cost. And David Sims might be her only hope.

CHAPTER TEN

She is back in her own place, their own place, in the tiny sitting room that is their new home. Rosa pops her chin up with one fist and pokes her tongue out of her pursed lips. She could be fourteen years old again, except the short red schoolgirl curls of the past are now fairer and flowing down her feminine angular shoulders. Her nose is still too small for the round face, but her freckles have become camouflaged against a fake tan. She laughs loudly but Emma knows it is fake. Then Rosa begins to dance, waving her arms in the air as she twirls around the dingy room. She kicks off her shoes even though they are flat, then unbuttons her blouse as if doing a striptease. Emma looks on without comment but can feel the blood boiling up inside. Why is Rosa acting like it is her own flat? Who does she think she is? Why is she always intruding into my life? Rosa forms a rare expression of seriousness for a few seconds as if hearing the silent questions asked about her. Suddenly a shadow splits the room in two. Emma turns to the source. It is Dan. But he is not looking at her. He is watching Rosa and his face is purple with fury.

***

Emma looks up at the man who claims to know her inside and out, the man who is no longer a stranger. Now he is David rather than 'that man'. It is funny how quickly she adapted to the situation once finally accepting it. After so many weeks alone in hospital, his relentless visits have forced her to feel a connection to him. Rather strangely he is looking less and less like someone of her parent's generation and Emma assumes it is because she is seeing the person behind the middle-aged face. The salt and pepper hair is no longer the first thing she looks at. Neither is the sagging skin above his eyes. Rather it is one of the more personal traits – walking tentatively towards her; dabbing his forehead with a handkerchief before he sits down; an unevenness of his eyes which is oddly attractive. More and more he is looking like someone she knows and the fear at the thought of him walking into the room has gone. Most surprisingly of all she's even beginning to look forward to his visits. On a more practical level, after successfully fending off the detectives he has now turned into a different kind of protector providing her with the basic needs of a hospital patient - clean clothes, toiletries, magazines and chocolate.

Things are getting easier so she tries to keep the term Stockholm Syndrome buried in the back of her mind. And the idea of him being her kidnapper is crazy because, somehow, she knows he would stop coming if she insisted. And she doesn't want that because he has a knack of reassuring her things will be okay. The only occasions when his composure slips are when she mentions Rosa, or the male detective who's been to the hospital at least twice that she's aware of. This is hardly surprising given his insistence that Emma does not get distressed. He wants her home as soon as possible. *Home.* She tells herself things could be a whole lot worse. David is smart, thoughtful, handsome and successful. Moreover, he is the only person with any inkling of her younger self, the woman before marriage, children and grandchildren. So, it is in her interest to keep him close.

There has been no further mention of Mrs Weekes, a mutual, undeclared, agreement that Emma knows is sensible. She hasn't dealt well with the elderly lady's deterioration and has decided it would be wise not to pursue the outcome any time soon. But this doesn't mean Emma has stopped asking questions about other people.

To her immense pain, Emma has heard about her parents' later lives from David. The couple remained in the family house until her father's death at sixty-nine. Emma's beloved father finally succumbed to heart disease, an illness it seems he'd had to endure for a long time. He'd been more or less housebound for years and reliant on his wife for many of his personal needs. Eventually, his beloved musical work was beyond him. This, David said, was the final nail in the coffin. Despite having people around who loved him dearly, Jonathan Watt, the successful, award-winning musician, was weary, frail and ready to leave the world.

Although able to care for her husband while he was alive, Jennifer Watt deteriorated rapidly after his death. David said it was as if her mind followed Jonathan out of this mortal realm while leaving her physically intact body behind. Emma, David and the other family members spent the next year rotating homecare duties, but the situation was deemed detrimental to the mental health of all involved. Therefore, the house was sold to pay for Jennifer's ongoing residential care.

Emma listens to the grim updates impassively though slightly bewildered that this near stranger has more memory of her parents than she has. He makes no mention of her father's criminal record probably because they both know this would have contributed to his deterioration. It is quite surreal to hear words like "heart disease", "hospice" and "dementia" without feeling depressed or bereaved, but Emma cannot relate to these events which happened two years earlier. It is as though Jon and Jennifer Watt are characters in a book rather than the two people she loves more than anyone else in the world. Or is it plain and simple that she's at the denial stage of grief?

She knows there is a recess in her mind still holding on to the hope that everything around her is an overrunning dream. That one thin hope is preventing her from breaking down completely. At the same time she needs to keep going, keep asking about the people she really cares about. But there would be no point in asking about Dan. How on earth could she mention a former fiancée to her current husband? No. Discovering Dan's fate will have to wait until later. Or perhaps Tina will come up with something

There is only one person left to ask David about. Unfortunately, he still refuses to discuss what he calls the distant past, meaning Rosa. "Not until you are better" has become a stock answer, convenient to him though frustrating to Emma. But it gives her even greater motivation to get well, to finally leave hospital. Because there is so much more to learn, as unpleasant as it may turn out to be. She hasn't forgotten the snippets of information David let slip during their conversation in the hospital courtyard.

It was a long time ago, and *it wasn't your fault.*

And there is another mystery to be solved. David is telling her that she disappeared from their anniversary party which was at the Seahaven boathouse near where they live. No one had noticed Emma was missing until two of the guests were leaving and they wanted to thank her.

'There were different groups of people scattered between the courtyard, the function room and the bar, so it wasn't strange that we didn't cross paths for so long.'

At our anniversary party? Emma wonders. She recalls the words of the detective,

Daniel Merriman was concerned about your whereabouts for about one hour before the sighting. But not David. 'So, what did you do when you realised I wasn't anywhere?'

He gives an ironic laugh. 'Nothing actually. I assumed you'd decided to go home for some reason, whether drunk or in a huff. It wasn't until I got back to the house and found it empty that I started to get worried.'

'But you saw me speaking to the woman at the boathouse so why didn't you think I could have gone with her?'

'Who told you that?'

'Er, I can't remember. So many people have been in here. Did you see me with her?'

He glances up at the ceiling for a few seconds before replying, 'Yes, at least I saw you leaving to talk to someone. It could have been a taxi driver for all I knew then.'

Female taxi drivers existed even in her day yet somehow Emma doesn't believe him. She knows there is no point in dwelling on this. 'So, finally, you called the police.'

'Yes, but they weren't interested. They said you were a grown woman, made several insulting comments regarding our marriage then told me to contact them again if you hadn't shown up in another twenty-four hours.'

'And?'

'So I contacted them again and they began looking around. It was the following day when reports came in of someone in the water. Shortly after, a helicopter picked you up.'

'But that's crazy. More than two days would have passed by then.' It is as though she is talking about someone else.

'Well, that's not important right now. They found you and that's all I care about.'

He doesn't comment on the elephant in the room – so many coincidences. Twenty-five-year anniversary parties. Emma disappearing from both before turning up in the sea. Two dead women ... perhaps. But both events are still only words spoken by other people as Emma cannot recall either death. But when she finally does remember, she is certain the first one will really hurt. For now, she focuses on the easiest one.

'David, do you know any more about the young woman who is missing? Are you still sure she's not dead?' For a few seconds, there is no response, but this silence speaks volumes. 'You have heard something, haven't you?'

Taking her hands, he inhales deeply before speaking. 'Yes, a young woman's body was found in a boat drifting at sea. The police haven't released more details regarding the identity, but I am more than certain it is no one we know.' The fact that Emma doesn't seem to know anyone is not mentioned.

Emma has to stop herself reminding him of what he said about his line of work. He clearly does not know everything. 'So, the detective wasn't playing with my mind at all, about her being dead and someone who looks like me photographed with her?'

He drops her hands. 'You never told me about a photograph.'

Didn't she? 'Well, apparently a security camera took it as we were getting into the boat. The image is blurred but Detective Carr is confident they can get a positive identification. It's crazy. Does he honestly think I killed some woman I don't know?'

Another upwards glance. 'Whatever he thinks, Darling, he is not coming within an inch of you until you are one hundred per cent recovered. He can talk to me instead.'

'But you're not the one being accused of killing her.'

'Oh, don't be ridiculous, Darling. You sound as if he's convinced you without any proof at all.' He rubs his temples as if in great pain.

'The man's an idiot. Either that or he's desperately searching for a crime where one doesn't exist.'

'But why would he do that? What would be the point of wasting his own time? And worse than anything else, it would be harming innocent people.'

'That doesn't cross the minds of men and women like him,' he says. 'They don't care who's innocent or guilty as long as they get their tarnished stripes. Yes, many police are as guilty as the crooks they are supposed to protect us from.'

Their conversation is getting further away from the mysterious victim, but it is a welcome distraction from what awaits them in another part of the hospital. However, the clock is ticking, and both know it is time to face the truth.

A new location and a new hurdle. Emma and David are waiting together outside a door at the end of a corridor. It is the blandest and most dismal place she has ever been in. The couple were given two options regarding this new referral.

They could either wait until the morning ward round or hang around the outpatient department until the end of the consultant's clinic. Emma couldn't have cared less but for David, it was a no-brainer. If something was wrong, the doctors needed to start treatment as soon as possible in case things got worse. There would always be private health care if need be.

His nerves are showing as he refuses to sit in the plastic chair even though it has just been wiped over with some ghastly-smelling liquid. In contrast, she is in a wheelchair, something she took a while to agree to, but the nurse insisted it was hospital policy. Emma doubts they would have been able to stop her if she'd gone ahead and travelled the few corridors and lifts by foot. In the end, she did it for David who seems to be a stickler for the rules. She wonders what made her marry such a man in the first place then remembers Dan was exactly the same. It seems after losing him she found a similar replacement. But was David second best? As if reading her mind David gives her shoulder a possessive squeeze.

After some hesitation, she forces herself to look up into his tired eyes. 'What's going to happen to me?' She makes a feeble attempt to smile not sure if she is genuinely worried or just going through the motions.

He crouches down and takes her hands in his. 'You are going to be fine, Darling. They'll just take a look at your head to make sure there's no bruising inside that could be causing the memory loss. And even if they find something, it'll heal in time.'

She wonders if it will. The thought of brain damage doesn't scare her. Rather it is the possibility of a complete recovery that she dreads most. For she isn't ready to deal with thirty years of memories engulfing her consciousness, even if they are real; especially if they are real. She would have to re-live the pain and grief that surely came before her accident.

A new thought comes to mind. Could these grim experiences have some connection to the incident at the boathouse? Did she try to kill herself? She could have paid that young woman to take her out to sea so she could drown, like Rosa. It wouldn't be impossible, but she accepts it's not likely. Middle-aged people are faced with the death of elderly parents all the time. Emma can remember her mother dealing with her own parents' deaths. Of course, she was devastated but she got through it. Life must carry on for those left behind.

However, there are two crucial differences between Emma and how her mother was at that time. Firstly, Emma doesn't feel middle-aged at all. In fact, she barely feels like a responsible and independent adult. Secondly, her most recent memories of both parents are of two fit and healthy people in early middle age. They are not sick or debilitated. She can still hear their voices, see their beautiful faces, feel the warmth of their hugs. And these sensations are hardly memories when it seems they were only experienced weeks ago, not years. Not decades.

At least brain damage would mean not having to experience the pain all over again, allowing her to wallow in the memories she does have, the memories she cherishes. It would be like one of those black-and-white films her mother loved to watch, where the heroine, struck down by amnesia, learns to love all over again. But she knows it isn't as simple as that. This isn't some movie or mystery book, is it? Someone doesn't just forget a huge part of their life. At some point in the future, in days, weeks or months, the truth will come crashing down on her; she's not sure how she will survive when it does. She feels the pressure of his hands on her shoulders bringing her back to the moment.

'You are coming back to me, aren't you?' His eyes are misty, and they penetrate Emma's own.

'I think so. I feel like I'm divided into two parts, the one here with you now and the other far away. But I am trying David.'

He leans over and kisses her on the cheek. She can smell his aftershave but this time it does not repulse her. On the contrary, her heart quickens, and this confuses her. Is she now attracted to him or merely scared of what is looming nearer? She pushes her head into his chest and feels his own heart beating as he kisses her hair while rocking back and forth. Then she pulls away and they sit in silence.

What she told David was the truth. She can feel part of herself becoming his wife, a transition which is providing her with some comfort in this terrifying new world. But deep down she knows that a comfort blanket is all that it is, and nothing more. She would give the rest of her life just for a few moments with her parents, with Dan. With Rosa.

There is movement behind the door and a tall, distinguished man enters the corridor. He isn't wearing a white coat or one of those odd scrubs. Instead, he wears a suit and tie, items of clothing that are at least as expensive as those David is wearing. As Mr Moneyworth steps to the side to invite them inside the consulting room. He looks graver than Emma feels, and she prepares herself for some terminal diagnosis. Is it cancer or heart disease? *Heart disease.* Has she inherited her father's illness as well as her mother's dementia? However, within seconds of being inside, the consultant neurosurgeon merely explains to Emma and David what they already know. She is to be taken for a brain scan and what happens next will depend on the results of the scan. If there is any suspicion of injury, she will be taken to surgery as soon as possible. If, however, the scan is normal, they will discuss further options with her and David.

'The orderlies will be here shortly to take you to the x-ray department. The scan is painless, but some patients feel a little disoriented while the pictures are being taken. There will always be a radiographer close by so you will not be by yourself. It is important that you keep as still as you can in order for us to have the clearest images. Do you have any questions?'

'If there is any brain damage, what happens then?' David takes hold of Emma's hand before she can move it away. The concern in his voice contradicts his earlier attempts to reassure Emma. She is touched by his obvious affection.

'We'll operate of course. How soon will depend on what we find. It may be a case that we can do nothing, so we leave things be.'

'But if there is something wrong, you must fix it or she'll never get her memory back.' He sounds desperate.

Dr Moneyworth gives a meaningless nod without replying. Emma observes the senior doctor's demeanour. Although appearing sympathetic, it is likely a look he's mastered over the past twenty years or so. And it's probably served him well. But he doesn't fool her. She can read his scepticism just like she can read that of every other member of staff. She doesn't blame them. There is no external bruising to suggest that she banged her head during the mysterious accident. Nor did she need to be resuscitated meaning that her heart did not stop beating at any time. This means it is unlikely she has brain damage.

And if there is no physical damage to her brain, it could only mean it's psychological or even a mental illness. So, what would happen to her then? If she told a psychiatrist her thoughts, they would say she was insane and section her. They wouldn't even bother with the scan. A sudden panic sets in and it comes from nowhere. She can't be locked away because it would put an end to any chance she had of finding out what happened to Rosa. And she suspects the answer probably lies with David.

It wasn't your fault.

CHAPTER ELEVEN

People are standing outside the austere building and shifting around awkwardly. Her mother and father are there, too. They are dressed in black. Everyone is wearing black. Even the clouds are darker than they ever were. Yet Rosa appears larger than life, her now strawberry blonde curls all that is vibrant amongst the gloom. Emma kisses her tear-stained cheek. It is the first time she has seen her best friend cry. Her only friend. She takes Rosa's hands in hers and squeezes them. They are ice cold. Her eyes are dead, too. There is a burning sensation in Emma's back and she turns to find Dan standing behind her. His expression is passive, but she knows he wants to leave. He doesn't have to say the words. Emma steps away from Rosa because it is too late to go back. The friends share a knowing look. Nothing will ever be the same again. Not for Rosa, not for Emma. Dan grabs her hand and is dragging her away from the freshly dug grave. Emma keeps turning back to look at her friend who is left alone with her grief. Rosa is standing in the same spot. Emma's hand is hurting as Dan grips it harder and harder, pulling her further and further into the darkness ahead.

***

The tea is almost undrinkable this morning. Is it a coincidence that the nearer Emma gets to leaving hospital, the worse the meals are? Before they were a means to survival so there was little point in disliking chips without salt and vinegar, mashed potatoes without heaps of butter, roast chicken without stuffing. She may not be a successful career person like Dan or David, but nobody would turn up their nose at her cooking, especially her Spaghetti Bolognese. She wonders if David eats it and she has to suppress a giggle at the image of sauce stains on his expensive ties.

'You seem happy this morning,' Tina says, observing this unusual expression.

'Oh just thinking back to the good times. Any luck with your investigation, Tina? I've been waiting a few days now.'

Pulling a disapproving face, Tina says, 'Well I'm not sure you deserve to know after hurting my feelings,' as she collects the full cup of tea and places it back on the trolley.

'Oh, I'm sorry but I didn't feel like a drink this morning,' Emma says quickly.

Tina laughs. 'Only pulling your leg. I just pour the milk and water. Anyway, I have got plenty of news, but you'll have to wait a bit longer... till the end of my shift. I'll pop back in about two hours so don't you go disappearing.' She winks before wheeling the trolley out of the room.

Emma is beginning to wonder if Tina is a bit of a fantasist and doesn't actually know any more than she does herself. Maybe the girl is more deluded than Emma, or just trying to impress her. Whatever the truth, it has forced Emma to reconsider her priorities. She's thought about Dan a lot the past few days, and, rather bizarrely this makes her feel guilty. Although not surprising given their close relationship, it is hardly the best way to continue her acclimatisation to her new world, and in particular, her new family.

It is David whom she should be wondering about and the young woman whose name she cannot remember for the life of her. Over the past few days, her feelings are shifting on some matters. The thought of being mother to a grown woman who is herself a mother is now less appealing than being the wife of a middle-aged man. Even though she hasn't accepted being middle-aged herself, there are thousands of women married to men two or more generations older. And it's not as if David isn't still a handsome man. She wonders if he will expect anything physical from her or if he has moved on to a younger mistress. Hopefully, he has. And what about her?

It is no good. Emma's mind returns to Dan, and her heart quickens as she imagines he is holding her in his arms. Maybe, just maybe. If Tina is telling the truth, what might she be about to tell her? Emma will have to steel herself for what will surely be a shock. She accepts Dan is probably married with children. Yes, of course, he is. Like David, he is a brilliant lawyer who no doubt owns his own legal practice. A wistful sigh escapes her lips as she remembers the times they shared.

Since living together, Dan had used Emma as a sounding board relating various aspects of cases to get an objective and unemotional opinion. And as far as she remembers, it worked well. She never sought to change his mind. Instead, she acted as a would-be juror telling him which points swayed her more than others. It also helped him organise his train of thought. Despite his demanding and impressive job, Dan had a muddled mind more suited to an artist than a slick lawyer. The notes he'd taken at meetings, undated and unnamed were often useless. Emma, on the other hand, had a photographic memory and her brain somehow retained all the information that went into it. They were the perfect partnership. Like the husband-and-wife television crime shows she grew up watching. He was the brilliant but accident-prone investigator; she the unpaid personal assistant, both organised and discreet.

How ironic to think of herself this way when she can barely remember her own name.

All of the other girls were surprised when Emma caught the eye of the best-looking boy in the school. Little did they know that he'd had a crush on her since the moment she walked into his classroom for the first time. It took him a few years to pluck up the courage to ask her out, but when she said yes, he promised to look after her forevermore. The proclamation was absurdly immature and naïve, but he stood by his word. He persuaded her to follow him to his university and accept any course that would take her.

On reflection, it was a mistake - three wasted years on her part. But he provided stability while she was drifting aimlessly after graduation. That was a difficult time for her, and she wore clothes to match her situation: scruffy jeans, t-shirts and trainers. It was an effort to put lipstick on. In contrast, Dan's path was mapped out after finding a place at the local law firm. It was the first rung of the ladder, and he climbed the next one quickly. He repeated his pledge to take care of her and, at the age of twenty-two, Emma agreed to move into his rented flat above the newsagents.

Their relationship was almost perfect albeit with its ups and downs. Despite being an absurdly handsome and intelligent man, Daniel Merriman was insecure about Emma's feelings for him. He was afraid that every day with her might be his last. His emerald eyes never locked with those of his many female admirers, the admirers who would snap him up if only he were single. Who wouldn't want to have that six-foot lean and athletic body protecting them, or that solicitor's wage providing for them?

More than that Emma loved him, and it was this fact itself which two people in particular found difficult to accept. Her mother for one; Rosa the other. Her mother was upset that her daughter's life seemed to be mirroring her own. Rosa was annoyed and hurt that she was losing her best friend. Things were never quite the same after Emma and Dan moved in together. How could they be?

The morning has seemed longer than a week and if there were a clock in the room, Emma is sure its hands would be turning backwards. She knows it's because she is waiting for Tina to return thus counting every second, like watching a kettle boil. Thinking of time she realises that she has no idea which month it is, or even the season. The constant temperature and lighting in the hospital keep patients in an unnatural atmosphere unaffected by the tilting of the Earth's axis. Is it spring, summer, autumn or winter? All she knows is her parents' party was in July but that means nothing now because thirty years have passed since then, not days or weeks. No. That was a moment in time, irrelevant and with no importance other than nostalgic worth.

Emma will have to search elsewhere for clues to gauge the current season. There is not much to help her, however. The staff wear the same uniform come rain, snow or shine, and David is always in a suit. It's like they are all in a state of suspended animation with everything slowed down almost to a stop.

Come on Tina!

Finally, the moment arrives. There's no rattling crockery or whirring trolley wheels to announce her arrival this time. Rather Tina's entry into the room is as silent as any cat thief especially as Emma didn't notice her coming through the door.

'Here I am,' Tina says, prising a folded sheet of paper from the pocket of her skin-tight jeans. No longer wearing the unflattering uniform, she looks even younger and prettier than before, with makeup on and sleek dark locks flowing over her cropped pink t-shirt. She reaches her bare arm out to Emma and deposits the sheet in her lap.

Emma flattens out the sheet and stares at the printed mess. 'Thank you,' is all she manages to say.

'Hope it's some help to you. Sorry, but I've got to rush,' Tina says quickly, before turning back to the door. She is no longer the patients' servant at the beck and call of their peculiar tastes, but an equal citizen wasting precious free time.

'What do you mean?' Emma scans the collage of squiggles, shapes and disconnected words not knowing where to begin. Disappointment seeps through her as she suspects she's been waiting around for nothing. After all, why would Tina's research come up with anything different to her own? Yet the words on the paper must mean something. 'Please don't go yet, Tina. I need you to explain this to me.'

The young woman stops and chews her lip in contemplation. 'My boyfriend's parked up outside so I can't stay long.' She takes back the paper and frowns. 'Oh my! I can barely make sense of it myself. Now let's see. Why did I put that in bold? Oh, dearie me.' She starts humming.

Feeling herself getting irritated Emma bites her lip, too. She doesn't understand why she is feeling this way all of a sudden especially when Tina has apparently taken so many risks to help her find Dan. Perhaps it is plain old jealousy, having to look at this gorgeous young woman with her prince waiting to pick her up in his carriage. Youth is beauty – that's what her mother always said when she saw someone younger and more attractive than her. It doesn't last, she would say with a smug expression. But despite partly coming to terms with her situation, Emma still feels robbed of her youth, and at this moment in time wants to take it out on the youthful woman who is helping her. She steels herself. 'Don't worry. Just tell me if you've found out where he lives.'

'Ah yes.' Tina places the sheet of paper on the bed. 'Prepare yourself for a surprise.'

'What do you mean? Where is he?'

'Well, your ex-boyfriend is certainly not a judge. He's not even a solicitor.'

It is a surprise. A shock even. That was the only career Dan ever considered. 'What does he do now?'

Tina laughs. 'Something far more interesting. Well actually, he's not got any job from what I could make out. Nor a house for that matter.'

No house or job. Suddenly Emma doesn't want to know. But she must. 'Oh no. Please don't tell me Dan's in prison.'

Tina laughs. 'I said interesting not infamous. He's living a nomadic lifestyle on a barge and sailing up and down the country.'

The relief lasts no more than a split second. 'A barge! Isn't that some sort of boat? How can he live on a boat?'

'Thousands of people do. You made Mr Merriman sound all suited up and stuffy but he's one cool guy.'

That is not the image Emma has right now. 'But how does he buy food and things if he doesn't work?' She knows these are the words of an older person who has long since abandoned any sense of romance and daring.

By now Tina is halfway out of the door. 'He's got some travel programme he puts out so I guess he gets money from advertising.

That's how most things work these days, isn't it? See you tomorrow!'

Emma has no idea how things work these days. All she knows is that Dan should be in a large, detached house not on a boat sailing up and down dirty canals. 'Wait!' she calls out. 'This still doesn't tell me where he is.'

Tina pops her head back into the room. 'I was going to tell you more tomorrow, but he's parked up in a marina for the next week. They do that every now and again. You can always find him if you want to.'

Emma has spent the past hour trying to decipher the notes but to no avail. Couldn't Tina have stayed a few more minutes to clear everything up? It is frustrating having to wait another day until the young woman can explain her findings, particularly as this leaves Emma at the mercy of her own thoughts. If Dan has his own tv show, does that mean he's famous? The man she loved and was going to marry could not have wanted anything less. He had little time for films and television saying he saw enough real-life drama to last him a lifetime. It was a rarity for him to be inside a cinema, usually on her birthday, and then he would pretend to fall asleep. But Emma suspects this was a childish way of belittling Rosa's achievements both in school and theatres. Acting was for people who couldn't make anything of their own lives, he would say. They are always trying to be someone else. It was so mean.

'What was mean?'

Not realising she said the words aloud, Emma jumps at the sound of another person's voice. She looks up to see David appearing slightly puzzled though smiling, and she is shocked to feel a pang of guilt hit her inside. 'Oh the ward sister made a student nurse cry earlier,' she says, keeping her eyes fixed on her hands. 'I felt so sorry for her.'

He chuckles. 'You wouldn't want to see me in court. I make witnesses cry all the time.'

The image of Detective Carr flashes through her mind on hearing the mention of courts and witnesses causing Emma to shudder. If there is one silver lining to the horrendous situation she has found herself in it is that she is married to a top barrister, one few people could afford to hire. After standing up she brushes imaginary creases out of her clothes.

'I bet you can't wait to change into something less comfortable,' he jokes.

Now it is Emma's turn to look confused, but then she can't help but smile. 'I know. If I never see a pair of leisure trousers again, it would be too soon.' The statement is true. Seeing Tina looking so svelte in her jeans and top earlier has instilled in Emma a need to prove she can still look attractive. She accepts that her own jeans and t-shirt days are past, but hopefully, she's inherited her mother's classy dress sense.

'Well let's concentrate on the here and now for a bit longer, just until we've got past ... ', his voice trails off as he picks up the sheet of paper on the bed. 'What's this?'

Dumbstruck, Emma can only watch as David pulls out pair of glasses from his inside pocket before frowning. 'Who gave you this, Emma?'

Emma. Not Em or Darling. She knows she cannot tell him the truth in case Tina has done something illegal, but what else can she say? At last, her mind clears. 'Oh, I did that the other day. The nurse suggested I use the library to get me out of this room.'

Her heart pumps wildly filling her cheeks with a red glow which screams out *I'm lying.*

Unfortunately, his mind seems to have already moved on. 'Why have you been looking up Daniel?' The tone is dispassionate but forceful.

'I didn't intend to but once I was on the computer, I couldn't find my parents or Rosa so the next person was Dan. It wasn't that I was looking him up really.'

He glances up before returning his focus to the paper in his hand. 'But not only did you look him up, Emma, but you also made notes on what he's been doing for the past thirty years. Not to mention where he is now.'

'Well, I was just curious about what he's been doing. I'd run out of people I could look up.'

'Did you not want to look up your own husband?'

There is nothing Emma can say so she merely drops her head in shame.

"He deserted you, Emma, left you when you needed to be looked after.'

It feels like the oxygen has been sucked out of the air between them and Emma can hardly breathe. The first time he mentions Dan, and it is to stab her in the heart with. They stand in silence not moving until a new voice breaks the spell.

They both look up to see a man standing by the door, his eyebrows raised and his lips pursed. 'Emma, is it?'

David gives the porter a terse smile. 'Yes, we are ready.' He crumples up the paper and puts it into one of the bins.

Chapter Twelve

They are in a restaurant but not alone. It must be a double date because there is another couple with them. David sits across the table and is smiling at her. There is a message in his eyes, but she cannot read it. His face is different. His dark hair shines as much as his coal-black eyes. The flawless skin on his face glows, too. He is young like her. She looks down at the table hoping to see her own reflection, her young reflection. She needs to see it. But the tablecloth blocks her view. Her gaze turns to the others at the table. Dan is not smiling. He is angry, but she does not know who with. Is it with her? She doesn't think so. No. It is most likely with Rosa because she is there too, pulling her usual false faces. Smiling, laughing, brooding. And Dan is always angry when he sees Rosa. A cork pops and a waiter pours wine into four glasses, but one overflows. Rosa leans forward and licks the falling drops in a suggestive manner. Emma is embarrassed for her friend who she assumes is very drunk. She looks at Dan. He shakes his head and then leaves the table. She turns to the side, but Rosa has gone, too. It is just Emma and David at the table. He is still smiling at her.

***

It looks like a rocket airlock, but she is not in outer space. At least she doesn't think so. Her heart rate matches the rising sense of panic she feels staring at the far too-narrow opening of the X-ray machine. How on earth do they expect anyone to spend an hour inside that? She tries to remember if she's ever suffered from claustrophobia but realises it wouldn't matter because there's a first time for everything. A man in a white boiler suit mutters something to her. His words are incomprehensible, but she assumes they are meant to be comforting. Then he disappears leaving her alone with her rising terror. For a few minutes, nothing happens and she wonders if the room itself is a giant X-ray and this is as scary as it will get. But then a whirring begins and the shelf she's lying on begins to slide her, head first, into the giant capsule. Clicking, grating, clanking. The medic warned her of the unsettling noise made by the scanner, yet Emma is grateful for the distraction which is helping to take her mind off this temporary state of immobility.

She dares not open her eyes in case the sight of her enclosed surroundings leads to absolute panic but she knows she is close to that point already. Try to think of something reassuring. David is waiting for her outside. They can leave the hospital as soon as the scan results are ready. But her heart continues to race so she thinks of something else. Dan or Rosa or her parents. If she could only concentrate on a specific moment in time, picture the setting, embrace every sensation, hear every sound, maybe she could get back there.

As she walks up the gravelled path, a muffled Schubert piano piece filters through the large Georgian window. She feels guilty interrupting such a timeless melodic sound with the trashy chime of the doorbell installed in the seventies. It is a welcome surprise to hear her father playing the instrument for pleasure these days, but she supposes this is something he chooses to do in his private moments. Usually, it is just a mishmash of notes played in various arrangements in the hope that he will happen upon a decent, not to mention original melody. This would be a rare and rewarding achievement these days, not that he needs the money anymore. Twenty years of successful film and television compositions mean that the royalties alone are more than enough to live comfortably on. But Jonathan Watt is always in search of his next masterpiece, and he has a new project to breathe life into his far too comfortable middle age.

He opens the door and smiles at the surprise visitor. Wearing fawn cords and a baggy grey jumper given to him as a Christmas present, he looks every minute and more of his forty-eight years. His hair is more salt than pepper, and his deep-set but still piercing eyes, framed by dark shadows, look like sapphires amongst the muddy pools of skin.

'Hi, Sweetheart. I'm afraid your mother isn't here,' he says, without moving.

Emma steps forward brushing past him. 'That's okay, Dad. Dan and I have just been for lunch and he's dropped me here as we were passing. Anyway, it's you I've come to see you.'

After closing the door behind her, Jonathan follows his daughter into the oversized kitchen and instinctively reaches for the kettle. Emma feels a pang of sadness observing her father as he spends some time working out the taps, then opening and closing cupboard doors without removing any of the contents. His demeanour is more that of a grandfather than a still youngish man. The shoulders that carried her as a child are now hunched; the hands that gripped her close to him now shake as they pour the tea. Why has so much changed in such a short period of time? Why do people have to get old?

'There you go, Luv. Help yourself to sugar.' He sits down opposite her on the rectangular kitchen island.

She nods without reminding him that she hasn't taken sugar in her drinks since she was fifteen. 'It was lovely to hear you playing the piano, Dad,' she says, carefully positioning her mug on the recently placed coaster.

A flash of red passes over his cheeks. Whether it is embarrassment or irritation, he looks like a man caught doing something he shouldn't. But the look is just a nanosecond, and he shrugs his shoulders before changing the subject. 'How was your lunch with Dan?'

'Oh, nothing to report home about. He just talked and I listened, as per usual.'

He grins. 'There's no shop talk when he's with me.' His expression turns more serious. 'I hope he doesn't get himself into trouble sharing confidential details with you.'

'Don't say that, Dad. I would never repeat anything he told me … not even to you or Mum.'

'That's my girl. He's doing very well in his career. I've heard he's up for a partnership.'

Emma nods. 'Yes, it's pretty much in the bag, apparently. Old Colson thinks the world of Dan and has all but anointed him as his successor.'

Jonathan glows with pride which causes a degree of bemusement in his daughter. Sometimes, she wonders if her father has transferred any aspirations he once had for her onto his future son-in-law. It might bother some people but not her. Dan is welcome to be the main breadwinner as far as she is concerned. She'd be happy to keep house forever.

A car engine rumbles outside and a minute later a voice calls through the front door glass. Emma looks at her father who shakes his head in confusion.

'Perhaps it's the postman,' she suggests, even though it is afternoon. 'I'll answer it.'

'No, no. You finish your tea. I'll go.' He touches her shoulder as he leaves the kitchen.

Through the kitchen doorway, Emma hears the front door opening followed by two male voices. One is her father's, the other is too muffled to distinguish. The door closes and both voices continue as they increase in volume. Then her father calls out, 'Luv, guess who's popped in, too. I hope you both didn't come here for a break from each other.'

Emma turns around to view her father's latest visitor, trying to quell any rising annoyance. He said he was going straight to the office after their lunch so what's he doing here? But her forced smile drops as the two figures emerge from the hallway. Because it is not Dan standing next to her father, but David, his face flushed and veins bulging from his forehead. Both hands are curled into fists as he steps towards her. He calls her name over and over, his voice gentle but his eyes full of hate. She cries out to her father, but he is no longer there. Why has he abandoned her? Now the light has gone, and darkness is all around her. All she can hear is her name. *Emma. Emma.* She must be dreaming.

Heat rises throughout her body even though the air around her is cold. It feels as if her blood is reaching boiling point and she opens her mouth to call for help but there is no sound beyond the cacophony of metallic clanks around her. Unable to move her head she attempts to use her hands and feet to call for help, but they too are frozen. Now her blood is hurtling through her heart like a runaway train ignoring what is ahead. She cannot possibly survive this experience and waits for the inevitable crash. Through her closed eyelids, the light is now blinding, but the sounds have ceased.

'You can open your eyes now.'

'So, I'll be over some tomorrow. David wanted me to come today but I said you would need time to get your bearings. Bye, Darling.' The woman's dark brown face erupted into a rehearsed smile as she waved through the tiny screen.

'Bye Thelma.' Emma handed the phone back to David for him to switch off. So, that was Thelma, her best friend. And the woman with whom she will have to go through this charade all over again. Catching up with her best friend who is also a total stranger. Another total stranger. Maybe, she can confide in her. Isn't that what best friends do? But maybe not tomorrow.

The bed she has lain in for months is now covered with several bulging holdalls. Emma wonders what is inside as she has worn little else but nighties and two different dressing gowns during her hospital stay. David has already consigned the well-worn nightwear to the bin, a decision which has her full backing even though she suspects it would not make any difference if she did object. In fact, David has taken full control of everything since her panic attack during the MRI scan.

'I should have been in there with her,' he'd shouted, as the radiology staff juggled with trying to calm Emma while pacifying him. He even tried to enter the X-ray room during the scan, but much to his fury was stopped at the door.

This mini drama resulted in security being summoned and a still half-delirious Emma wondering if her husband's anger was more about power than concern for her wellbeing. Although grateful to be out of the scanner, part of her wished she was back in her dream, at least until the moment David showed up in it.

As she expected, the scans showed no evidence of brain damage or any other abnormalities, so Emma's mental health was the next thing to be looked at. But to her surprise, David's enthusiasm for a precise diagnosis quickly evaporated. Whereas only days ago he was demanding more tests, he is now telling the doctors that his wife is better, and they will leave the hospital immediately. Emma supposes he is more scared of an illness he cannot understand than one that surgical instruments could fix. Or maybe ashamed. He would prefer to deny its existence or treat it as an idiosyncrasy — in the privacy of their own home. The medical staff do not seem to mind.

Now Emma must face up to her future with a man who is essentially a stranger. The only details she has are those he has given to her himself: he is a lawyer; his secretary's name is Lala; he is allergic to prawns. But none of these are facts she remembers herself. However, some memories are beginning to return. University for one. Yes, she did complete a degree although details such as location and subject have yet to materialise.

There are several stronger memories, memories of loved ones, yet, apart from the double date and scanner nightmare, David isn't in them. Nor are any other members of her new family. Instead, they are filled with Dan, Rosa, her mother and her father. And the memories are so clear it's as if she is really there with them all existing in the same time and space, breathing the same air. They seem so much more than flashbacks. Then she looks at David as he closes the travel bags and lifts them all with one hand as he holds out the other. He is not a memory, nor a figment of her imagination. He is without a doubt real. She takes his hand.

As each car approaches the hospital entrance, Emma braces herself for the first step inside her new life. At least everything looks familiar. Big, small, old, new, the vehicles seem no different to those from thirty years earlier but she's not sure she would notice the difference if they did. She's never been a car person.

There is a short line of taxis to the left and the driver at the front leans his head out of the window and stares at Emma. Wearing so much gold and dressed in a long cashmere coat she must look like a woman with a purse filled with cash. She hadn't wanted to put all the jewellery *back on* but David said it would get her in the right frame of mind.

"We're leaving the sick version of you in hospital," he said as if twenty-four-carat gold was a panacea for all illnesses.

At last, she sees a car making directly for her, and she takes a deep breath in preparation. It is rather surprising to witness the vehicle as it veers towards the entrance. She was expecting David to drive something flashy and expensive, but this car is shabby and dented at the side. It feels wrong. The car stops and the driver gets out. It is Detective Carr. His lips are curled upwards as if smiling but his eyes are stone cold.

'Emma Sims, I am arresting you for the murder of – ' 'Get away from her.' David is running towards them having left his car in the queue with its engine still running. 'My wife has literally taken her first step out of hospital in three months. This is outrageous behaviour even by your standards.'

Detective Carr pulls a sheet of paper from his jacket pocket and hands it to David. 'It is totally normal to arrest a suspect in a murder investigation, Mr Sims. Now if you would let things take their course. You are welcome to accompany your wife to the station.'

David is scanning what appears to be an arrest warrant after snatching it from Carr. A vein is bulging on his forehead giving the impression that one way or another he is about to explode. It is an image that unsettles her, as it resembles the one in her dream. And perhaps because she has seen it many times before. A shiver runs through her as she realises that she does not know the man taking her away from the hospital bubble which has provided her with a level of safety. He could be a possessive bully. After all, he is always ordering people around, and never taking advice from the medical staff like other relatives. Even worse, what if he beats her, just like Rosa's father? Memories of Mrs Jones's bruised face and hands come back to her flashing like warning signs. If she really did disappear from that boathouse, maybe she was trying to leave him. Maybe he followed them. Maybe he killed ... stop it, Emma. He is the barrister, not the criminal.

Meanwhile, the two men continue to lock horns, Emma once again merely a witness, and she wonders who will end up the victor. Behind them car horns sound and other men's voices join in the disturbance until David and the plain- clothes policeman are surrounded by furious motorists. The line of cars stretches back the entire length of the hospital grounds. Emma gazes over at the taxi driver who is still staring at her. In spite of the distance between them, she is certain he is grinning. For a few seconds, she considers jumping in his vehicle and telling him to just drive as fast as he can away from the melee. But Carr's tatty estate car remains at the front of the queue so they would be lucky to get out of the pickup area. Now people are stepping forward, some attempting to calm the situation, and Emma can no longer see what is happening. Without any forethought, she turns around and runs back through the hospital concourse.

What are you doing? There is no way out. You have to go back. But her instinct has overcome any sense of reason and is driving her away from the two men who want to take her with them.

Two flights of stairs lead up to a long corridor filled with patients and staff. She is still running but nobody cares because they are getting on with their own business. But behind someone is calling her name. He is getting closer. Turning around she sees anonymous men, women and children walking in opposite directions then the blond crown of Carr's head weaving through them. He is going to catch her. She hears a bell, and a lift door opens next to her. Jumping inside she presses any button and stands back. Oliver Carr appears and almost walks past the lift but then stops suddenly. He sees her just as the doors begin to close. 'Wait!' he shouts. 'Stop the lift!' Then he disappears.

As she watches each floor number light up, Emma feels like she's in an amusement arcade, playing a slot machine. When should she press the stop button? It's win or lose. Do or die. The decision is taken out of her hands when the lift, having reached the summit, begins to descend once again. The doors open at last. LG is lit up. Lower Ground. She steps out of the lift into a cold and dingy corridor leading two ways. To the left, she can hear a trolley being wheeled away from her. Is that the way to the morgue? She shivers at the thought of being close to so many dead bodies and heads off in the opposite direction.

Every few yards or so a young man or woman pass her but not one glances at the trespasser. Emma guesses they are student doctors and nurses, and this proves correct when she emerges outside a small block of flats. Different sirens are blaring all around and she dives through a gap in a hedge just before a police car passes behind her. At last, finding herself on a narrow footpath, she feels able to stop and catch her breath. After peering around the gap she has just jumped through, she is satisfied that the detective lost her some way back. But the rest also gives her a chance to reassess the situation.

Does she really want to become a fugitive in an alien world filled with strangers? She pictures David and Detective Carr in a race to find her. The longer she stands here, the more likely one of them succeeds. At least the decisions would be taken out of her hands. Decisions. These past few weeks she has had no say over her life, but this has been strangely comforting. The thought of being in total control of events is terrifying. She can't remember a time when she was. It was always her mother, father, Dan. Now David ... or Detective Carr. She brushes the leaves and dirt from her coat, and heads towards the sound of traffic keeping going until almost running into a bus. After one last glance behind her, she gets on it.

CHAPTER THIRTEEN

Emma is on a busy high street. She has no idea why she is there or where she is going. To her right are so many shops, so many fast-food restaurants, so many people. To her left, cars and taxis and red buses. She realises it must be Oxford Street. A man brushes past nearly knocking her off her feet which makes her angry so she shouts after him. But he does not care. She thinks she is there by herself but, when she turns back to resume her journey, she can see her mother walking towards her. At least she thinks it's her mother, but she looks different. Her cherry red lips match the wide belt pulled tight against her flat waist. But she never uses that shade of lipstick or style of clothes. Even the jewellery has changed. The delicate silver chains are gone, replaced with cheap and gaudy costume jewellery. Emma wonders why her mother has altered her appearance and decides to ask her once they reach each other. But as her mother approaches, it is clear that she is not looking at Emma but straight ahead. Emma stops dead and watches as her mother drifts past, either deaf to her daughter's calls or choosing to ignore them. Perhaps she is not really there, just a ghost of the past. Or the future. Then she is gone, and Emma continues on her way, her cheeks soaked with tears.

***

'Do you wish to buy a ticket, Madam?' The brittle voice somehow manages to boom through the narrow gap in the plastic window. It is a sign of the ticket officer's irritation at the travellers who keep him in a job.

'Yes. A single ticket to London, please.'

'That'll be one hundred and fifty pounds,' he says, pushing his palm under the gap.

'How much?' Up until that moment Emma had no idea how much a train ticket cost because she hasn't been on one for thirty years. She opens her purse and stares at the notes and coins inside. There is no need to count them.

'Well! Do you want the ticket or not?'

'Er, I don't have enough cash on me.' This is no time to be proud.

'We do take cards too,' he says, glancing downwards.

Emma nervously follows his eyes to the card inside her purse and then to the miniature cash machine on the counter. She can feel someone breathing over her shoulder and tutting from further back as well as sensing the dagger looks from the ticket man. Heat rises up into her cheeks and she thinks she might combust. Why didn't she write down the pin number?

It's no good. She will have to hitchhike. The thought almost makes her laugh out loud. What would her mother and father say? That's it!

Each digit is the birth month of your mother, father and you in that order.

Somehow it takes her three goes, first getting her mother's birth month wrong, then her own. She puts it down to concussion and, after climbing on the newly arrived train, breathes a huge sigh of relief. For the first time in this nightmare world, she is the person in control of her life. And she knows exactly where she wants to go.

Oxford Circus is as insane as she remembers it being, the same clash of workers, shoppers and tourists all caught in the same flow of human traffic. No sooner has she emerged from the underground station, she is almost knocked off her feet by one commuter in a particular hurry. Another one elbows her in the ribs to make enough room for himself. It must be lunchtime. London is living up to the bad reputation that Emma had assigned it in her past existence. No wonder she hated visiting Rosa after she moved there. Not that Rosa invited her that often.

Emma recalls the times when she stayed at her friend's tiny bedsit. She is certain that she went there several times at least because she can visualise the room to the smallest detail. It was smaller than her parent's hall. There was a single bed under a window that rattled even in summer. Along one wall was an assortment of miniature kitchen utensils - fridge, cooker, microwave. Even

the sink was smaller than average with a maximum load of two
tea plates and a few forks. It didn't matter as Emma doubts Rosa
bothered cooking for herself. It was as much as she could do to
eat anything at all. As for guests, her hostess skills amounted to a
guided tour of the nearest pizza restaurant or kebab shop. For an
aspiring actress, there was no time to worry about a balanced diet.
And there was no one else around to take care of her.

Following Rosa's departure for drama college, her mother was
convicted of manslaughter after stabbing Rosa's father. Everyone
knew it was more likely to have been self-defence given the fact
that Eddie Jones was a bully and a wife-beater. But Rosa's mother, wracked with misplaced guilt, could provide the jury with no
reason to doubt the prosecution's version of events. She was sen-
tenced to ten years in prison, leaving Rosa also suffering guilt for
not visiting her home more often. Being an only child she bore the
full weight of grief, shame and upheaval. She desperately needed
emotional support but there was none on offer, at least as far as
Emma is aware. It certainly didn't come from her.

Unfortunately, it was an awkward time for their friendship.
Emma was getting serious with Dan, and he didn't like her going
out with friends, particularly Rosa. She knew Rosa was hurt but
told herself that was life. First, there is family, then friends, then
lovers, then family again. It is the circle of life.

And they must have remained friends because Rosa was in the
garden preparing for the party. Or was that just a dream? At last,
Emma nears the end of the crazy mile that is Oxford Street and
turns into a slightly less busy road. She looks up at the faceless

offices and immediately thinks of her mother. While working in the London office, Dan claimed to have seen Mrs Watt walking along Oxford Street by herself. Although he tried to catch up with her, she disappeared into one of the indistinguishable entrances. According to Dan, she looked more glamorous than usual, including her lipstick being bright red rather than coral. But Emma thought he was stirring as a way of getting his own back. Jennifer Watt never approved of their engagement saying that her daughter was too young to settle down and should travel the world first. 'I know what I'm talking about," she would say any time Emma mentioned wedding plans.

Her parents married in their early twenties, a spontaneous act while travelling in the United States. The young couple were deeply in love having met as university students three years earlier. According to everyone who knew them, theirs was the most enviable and perfect of relationships, and a wedding was a way to endorse this view. But of course, perfect relationships don't need to be endorsed through marriage. At least that would come to be Jennifer's view. The romantic and sexy wedding was quickly followed by a mortgage and a baby.

However, they never endured the hardships experienced by so many families starting out. Jonathan, a talented musician, achieved immediate success with his piano compositions. The family moved out to the coast, the serenity of which was more amenable to his work. Jennifer never needed a paid job. Young Emma wanted for nothing except a sister or brother finally settling for the close companionship both friends and boyfriends offered.

But the loved-up couple were transformed by the comfortable life money brought them.

Her father spent most of his time locked away in his home studio, one of the sitting rooms, while her mother did whatever kept women did. The couple seemed to spend so little time together Emma always worried her parents had fallen out of love and would get divorced or fall out of love. Just like Rosa's parents.

That never happened. But now the older and wiser Emma recalls Dan's anecdote with the benefit of hindsight. Where was her mother going that day? Why was she more dressed up, her whole appearance more glamorous than her usual classic look? Her mother was going somewhere, no doubt, without her husband's knowledge. Something Emma is doing, too. She wonders if it was the same street she is walking down now.

There it is. It could be any old tenement building but for the large billboard over the canopied entrance. Emma is disappointed. She used to imagine Rosa treading the boards within some celebrated three-hundred-year-old theatre, not a grimy Victorian block. Perhaps it's all in the interior, she tells herself. But once inside she is more disillusioned still. There is no foyer as such, rather a dark wooden desk in front of a standard-sized door serves as both ticket office and reception. A young woman polishing pinned-up photographs is the only other person in sight. On noticing Emma, she stops and smiles.

'The box office doesn't open until the matinee finishes.' She looks up at a walled clock. 'It'll be another hour.' She continues polishing until realising the visitor hasn't moved. 'Is there anything else I can help you with?'

The stress of making the train and then finding the theatre has used up all of Emma's mental energy. She hasn't prepared for any questions she might face once she actually reached her destination, least of all from a cleaner. An awkward silence descends between them while the young woman waits for some sort of response. Nervously Emma looks past her at the displays hoping for inspiration. It comes.

'May I have a look at the photographs?'

The other woman smiles again. 'Of course. I hope you don't mind the smell of polish.' She turns back to her task.

Emma steps forward with intent. She knows exactly what she is looking for amongst the hundreds of faces frozen in times which are now in the past, some long past. Immediately, one image, in particular, holds her attention: a man wearing a top hat, with cheeks rouged, and kohled eyebrows. His eyes seem to move slightly as if still full of life rather than a splodge of chemicals on paper. But it is just a shadow passing across the display. She continues along the wall until reaching the end.

'It shouldn't be long now.'

Emma jumps. She's been so absorbed in the photographs she forgot about the other woman. 'Oh thank you. But I'm not here to buy tickets. It's more ... I mean ... I was wondering about an old friend of mine. She was here for a while. I was wondering if anyone remembers her.'

The young woman stares at Emma. 'Okay. What's her name?'

'Rosa Jones.'

A blank face. 'I'm sorry. That name means nothing to me. But I've only worked here five years so if she was here before –'

'Thirty years ago.' Emma is shocked at the force of her own words. She quickly softens her tone. 'Rosa had some acting roles here in the early nineties. Is anyone still around from back then?'

The woman laughs. 'Only the caretaker. I think he's been here since the eighteen-nineties.'

'Oh!' Emma wants to scream with excitement. In her wildest hopes, she imagined talking to a director or actor who worked with Rosa but knew deep down that was verging on the fantastical. Even if there were some old luvvie around from way back when, why would they speak to her? But a caretaker might. 'Is he here now?' Emma says, before holding her breath.

'He's always here. Do you want me to see if he's free?' 'Yes, please. Will you tell him it's important?' Emma knows she will have to justify that statement if the man agrees to see her. But she'll cross that bridge when, or if she comes to it. For now, she crosses her fingers.

Len Dawkins looks as old as the building that houses the theatre he's worked in so diligently over several decades. Emma tries to picture his grey-lined face as it was thirty years ago when the white hair had colour, the skin some suppleness and the spine was straight. She decides he must have looked old even then. Beneath the gnarled exterior, however, he is eloquent and charming, and Emma is surprised to see a man such as he buried away at the back of the modest establishment. But from the beginning of their chat, it is clear he holds the theatre in great esteem and takes immense pride in the role he's played.

They are sitting in the caretaker's office: a store cupboard with one wooden chair and a table holding a tray filled with tea-making necessities. Emma sits in the chair listening to Len as he gives her a history of the theatre with anecdotes added. Although she suspects some stories are embellished for effect, this does not detract from the enjoyment. It doesn't surprise her to learn that Len himself was once an aspiring actor.

'It was good while it lasted,' he says, with no hint of regret in his voice. 'But in this job, I've earned far more over these past thirty years than I would have done as an odd-job clown.' Emma believes him while doubting he ever played a clown.

Modesty is yet another one of Len's qualities. She could only imagine the life of a struggling actor: spending every spare minute in low-paid jobs just to cover the rent; trampling over friends and rivals for auditions only to suffer rejection at the first, or worse, final hurdle - the casting couch! For the vast majority, the struggle ends with the dashing of a lifetime's hopes and dreams, a far cry from the silver screen adulation reached by the very few.

At last, Len reaches the end of his monologue and, putting down his mug scratches his snowy white head. 'Have I seen you before somewhere?'

Suddenly nervous, Emma sips her tea while trying to forget about the stained crack in the cup. 'Perhaps you have,' she says. 'I may have come here once before with Rosa. We were best friends.'

'Ah yes. Lovely Rosa,' he says, his eyes glazing over with nostalgia at the mention of the name. Is it for Rosa or a time when he still possessed hopes and dreams of his own?

'So, do you remember her well?' she says, aware of the implication of an affirmative answer to her question.

But if Len is aware of Emma's part in Rosa's death, he shows no indication of it. 'Rosa was special, a star in the making, in the ascendancy. She had a fire in her eyes that lit up the stage with as much intensity as any spotlight.'

'Was she really that good?' Emma listens patiently while Len rhapsodizes over her friend. But it is not providing her with the right answers. ''But her roles hardly reflected that, did they?' She knows she needs to choose her words carefully. 'Rosa was already twenty-three by the time she died. I know it's wrong, but doesn't it get harder to win acting roles once you hit thirty, especially if you are a woman.'

He shrugs his shoulders as if personally offended. 'It's difficult for men, too, you know. There's always somebody younger waiting in the wings.'

Emma changes tack. 'Do you think Rosa had enough enthusiasm for the acting world?'

Len nods his head. 'Oh yes, she certainly did, at least in the beginning. Out in California, she fought like a wildcat to get a part.'

A memory comes back to Emma. Yes, Rosa did spend time in the States with her theatre group. The two friends joked about her travelling all the way to California only to end up in Silicon Valley, a far cry from Hollywood. Ironically, Rosa loved her experience in the technology mecca. *It's like stepping into the future, Em. I had to keep reminding myself I wasn't on some sci-fi set. They are so far ahead of us, it's unbelievable. I didn't want to leave.*

He sighs to himself. 'If it wasn't for that incident, she'd still be there now in my opinion.'

'Which incident was that?' Emma asks.

He looks at her curiously. 'You said you were her friend.' 'Yes, but I've had some issues with my short-term memory.' As soon as she finishes the sentence, she knows it doesn't make sense. But she is developing a knack for covering up her mistakes. 'It's beginning to affect my long-term memory, too.'

'Ah, I see. Say no more love,' he says, with a wink before getting back to Rosa. 'Poor thing had her drink spiked. Ended up in hospital. She wasn't in there long as it turned out, but by the time she recovered the tour was over. I honestly believe she'd have found a way to remain out there if she'd had more time. Such a shame. Once we got back to London, she seemed to lose heart in the profession. Seemed to lose the hunger.'

His last statement rings true. In her mind, Emma recalls that change in enthusiasm. One minute Rosa was as ambitious as any character from Fame, the next she hardly mentioned acting. She spent more time than ever coming back home. Yet the sparkle had not left her eyes. If anything, they shone more brightly than ever in those past few months that Emma can remember. 'Was she seeing anyone?'

Len's eyes widen. 'A bloke, you mean?' 'Well yes. Or a woman, I suppose.'

Another shake of the head. 'To tell you the truth there was no time for romance and all that nonsense. If needs must you got it where you could. Boyfriends, girlfriends or whatever, though, they came a poor second. Although there was one young man, Joe I think his name was. They hung around together quite a bit so there was probably more to it than friendship. He was pretty keen on her as I remember and asked Rosa to go travelling with him. I guess she turned him down because he went off by himself. After that if Rosa had anyone special in her life, as her friend you'd know better than anyone.'

Emma grimaces. Len is clearly seeing through the menopause excuse that he himself assumed. Hoping he isn't noticing her squirming, she continues. 'To be entirely honest with you, we fell out towards the end. She certainly never mentioned this Joe. If she had, I would have encouraged her to go with him, even if just for a short time. I couldn't understand why she kept coming back home, especially while she had no family there.'

'Ah, yes. To lose both parents together in that way was particularly tough,' he says. 'That driver should have got life.'

'What driver?' Emma asks.

'The one who ran them over. Rosa said he was doing well over the speed limit, yet he only got a couple of years ... for killing two people.'

Emma cannot believe that Rosa told people both her parents were dead. Was she so ashamed of her mother being in prison that she would rather deny her existence? Obviously, she was. A stab of guilt hits her in the chest. She was the only person Rosa could turn to, but Dan kept pulling her away. Poor Rosa. Compared to her own life, Emma's must have seemed heaven-blessed.

'I take it you know about her parents,' Len says, with a touch of doubt in his voice.

'Yes, of course. It was terrible. I mean we were still friends because she came to my parents' anniversary party. It's just that we were drifting apart by then. That's why I'm here, to find out what Rosa wasn't able to tell me herself, at least as much as I can.'

'It's a bit late for reconciliation though. I suppose I could give you the phone number of a medium who performs here sometimes. He's a bit of a fraud though.'

It is a relief to laugh. 'No thanks. I don't believe in the supernatural either. I guess it's just that, all of a sudden, I miss her.' This is all too true.

A sound of muffled applause signals the end of the matinee and their tête-à-tête. Emma stands up and thanks him for the tea and chat. It has been more useful than she could have dreamt. To her surprise, he holds out his hand which she shakes with some embarrassment. It is a formal end to what has been a rather intimate meeting. He opens the door and stands back to allow her to exit first. As she walks past him, he speaks once more.

'I hope you find the peace you're searching for.'

Emma smiles and thanks him again. She recognises a hint of mischief in his eyes and knows that they have indeed met before.

CHAPTER FOURTEEN

Emma watches as Rosa pushes the drawing pin into her left palm while being careful not to pierce a vein. It is Rosa's lucky pin, one that she stole from a theatre noticeboard. All actors have their peculiar strategies for dealing with audition nerves, and this is hers. After sucking away a tiny bubble of blood, she steps onto the stage and into the spotlight. There is no sound, not even a cough or rustle of paper. It is as though the entire audience is holding its collective breath, but that is not why it is silent. She stares out at the rows of empty seats before focusing on the blurred figure at the front. She waits for her cue. It comes in the form of a single gesture – a pointing finger. A deep breath later she is transported to another place: a New Jersey apartment, eyes welled with tears, her body rigid with terror. At this moment in time, Rosa no longer exists. She is someone else, a fictional character that has occupied her brittle shell. Ten minutes later satisfied with her performance, she bows. The blurred figure is clapping wildly.

Then the lights go on. Rosa jumps off the settee and hugs Emma. Now they are both covered in blood.

***

The sun is low in the sky signalling the day's end, and with it comes a drop in temperature. Once again commuters are rushing in all directions, this time towards various underground stations and their long and expensive journeys home. But Emma has no home to go to. She is both hungry and thirsty and is tempted by one McDonald's type restaurant after the other, but her priority must be to find somewhere to spend the night. After turning down a side street, the buildings change in both character and purpose. Banks, offices and flats take the place of the shops and, after walking another hundred yards or so, she walks into the first hotel she comes across.

Immediately the hustle and bustle of the metropolis make way for an eerie silence for which she is unprepared. Beneath her feet a deep pile carpet cushions any potential noise of footsteps and luggage in the large lobby, providing an odd place of relaxation for what are assumed to be hotel patrons unwinding with a drink or two.

Emma's eyes are drawn to a man dressed in a gold-braided uniform. He is staring at her, and she has to fight the urge to flee for the second time that day. If only she'd managed to grab one of those travel bags before bolting earlier. Feeling the blood rushing to her cheeks, she is relieved when the receptionist calls her over to the desk.

With a warm smile, the woman says, 'Good evening. Do you have a room booked?'

'Oh ... no ... actually, I've found myself stranded here until tomorrow.' Emma hates that she feels the need to explain herself to the attractive receptionist. Maybe it's because the way she is made up, with a sleek black bun, austere two-piece and piles of foundation cream, gives her a gravitas beyond her youthful age. In contrast, Emma has literally been through a hedge backwards.

The young receptionist, stretching her crimson lips wide apart, says, 'So, you need a room for tonight, is that correct?'

'Yes, it is. Could I have a single room, please?'

'I'm afraid we don't do single rooms, but I can offer you a small double.'

'Yes, that'll be fine.'

'Do you have your passport, Madam?'

'Er, no sorry. I'm not a tourist. That's why I don't have any luggage. You see, I - '

'That is not a problem, but you will have to pay for the room now rather than on departure. Is it for one night only?'

Emma doesn't know herself but decides to play it safe. 'Yes, for now. I might need to stay longer,' she says, before remembering she has no luggage. It doesn't matter because the receptionist is only paying attention to the answers she's asked for.

'That will be two hundred and sixty pounds,' she says. 'Are you paying by card?'

Two hundred ... But this time Emma doesn't panic. Instead, she calmly takes out the bank card and pushes it into the machine. 'Do you do evening meals?'

The receptionist does not seem to hear the question as there is no reply. A few seconds later she looks up from the machine. 'Madam, I'm sorry but this card is not going through. Is there another one you could use?'

Emma stares at the card being handed back to her. 'Oh, I probably put the wrong number in. I'm always doing that,' she laughs. 'Let me try again.'

But this time the receptionist isn't smiling. 'I'm afraid that would not make a difference, Madam. Do you have another means of payment?'

'Just let me try it again. I'm allowed three goes.'

'Madam, this card cannot be used.'

'Why not?'

Tilting her dark head to the side, the young woman's crimson lips mouth the answer. 'It has been blocked.'

Emma is numb and cannot answer. In fact, she's forgotten the original question she was asked. Around her people are moving and talking but she is frozen to the spot. By the time she comes to, the receptionist is talking to another member of staff behind the counter. He then turns to face her and, minus any subtlety, widens his eyes and nods his head. Without another thought she walks away from the desk and towards the hotel door, passing the man wearing the gold epaulettes who is still staring at her.

She runs back down Oxford Street, pushing past others as aggressively as any commuter on their way to or from the office. Unlike them, however, she has no destination in mind. All she wants is to put that hotel far behind her along with the heavily made-up receptionist and gold-epauletted man. Only when her bursting lungs and flailing legs can bear no more does she step into a doorway to recover her breath. Beads of water are running down her forehead and for the first time she notices it is raining, not heavily, but the dark clouds above suggest much worse is to come.

Somehow she has drifted away from the busy thoroughfares and into one that could be any rundown high street in any British town. Gone are the souvenir shops, tourists and hotels; in place are mostly boarded-up buildings with only a smattering of functioning businesses in between – a bookies, a pub and, rather curiously, a jewellery shop.

Counting the money in her purse she toys with the idea of trying one of the first two as a last hurrah before giving herself up. At least the pub would be dry. After wiping the rain from her face she crosses the narrow road towards the smell of stale ale before stopping to read a sign in the jeweller's window: WE BUY AND SELL GOLD.

A bell tinkles above her as she steps inside the tiny shop and onto a well-worn carpet. There is barely room to manoeuvre between the disorganised piles of furniture, ornaments and piles of crockery. On every wall are various shaped and sized clocks, the largest with pendulums creaking in disharmony. Bar a huge open ledger book, the glass counter is bare, but underneath are dozens of shallow wooden trays filled with an assortment of gold, silver, and precious stones. There is something oddly endearing about the cluttered shop. Emma could easily be back in her grandparents' time rather than thirty years ahead of her own.

An elderly man's head pokes out from behind a beaded doorway and shouts, 'We're closed, Dear.'

Emma points to the closed sign still facing inwards. 'I'm sorry but it says – '

'Well, I'm saying ...' He stops midsentence as he peers at her through metal-rimmed bifocals. 'I suppose, if it won't take long ... what is it you're after?'

'Oh, I'm not looking to purchase anything. It says in the window you buy gold.'

'I might do. It all depends on the gold. And I'll need some identification.'

Her heart drops. She even left the blocked credit card in the hotel. 'I haven't got any I'm afraid. Could you just give me something for these?' She takes off her necklace and earrings slamming them down on the glass counter. Noticing him staring at her rings she removes them, too. 'How much for all this?'

The proprietor doesn't speak as his wrinkled eyes scan her face, and then his hand reaches under the counter before re-emerging with a pocket magnifier. Emma watches in both anticipation and surprise as the man picks up each item in turn taking merely seconds to examine all. She holds her breath when he puts the magnifying glass back under the counter.

'It's good quality stuff,' he says, almost to himself.

'So, you'll take it?' she says, not bothering to hide the desperation in her voice.

But he shakes his head. 'I would, but I've already banked most of today's takings and I wouldn't want to offer you lower than the going rate.'

Emma looks over at the wooden cash register behind him. 'What could you offer?'

He turns to the side and smiles. 'There's nothing in that old thing. It's all on my person.' He pads his brown overall pocket and takes out a small roll of bank notes. After unravelling the notes, he lays them out on the counter. 'Three hundred pounds.'

Three hundred pounds sounds like a lot of money but Emma knows it would barely cover the cost of a train ticket to London or a night in a midrange hotel. She needs to think about this, but the clock hands are now almost deafening. Now the chimes start. She looks at the culprit timepiece which reads six o'clock.

'Three hundred pounds for all that?' She sighs knowing she should come back the next day to get the best price but that would mean finding another hotel. Just as she is about to agree, an idea comes to her. She picks up the wedding ring. 'If I take this back, would you still offer me three hundred for the rest?'

The man scratches his oiled-back hair and chews his lip in thought. 'I suppose that's fair. So, is it a deal?'

Of course, it is a deal. Not bothering to wait for a receipt she thanks him, puts the money in her bag, and threads her way back through the jumble of junk and collectables. Just as she is about

to open the door to leave, she hears him mutter something. 'I'm
sorry. What did you say?'

'I said, just a minute.' Then he rummages in his trouser pocket
and pulls out another few notes. 'Here's an extra fifty for the ring.
Take it or leave it.'

Taking the wedding ring back off her finger, she hands it to
him in exchange for the extra fifty pounds. Like the marriage, the
ring means nothing to her, but the money might make all the
difference.

As he hands her the notes, he holds his grip for a bit longer than
necessary causing her to look up in confusion. 'You're on the run,
aren't you?' he says.

She freezes. 'What do you mean by that?'

'From your husband.' He winks, releasing his hold on the cash.

She forces a smile and puts the money in her coat pocket before
leaving the shop as the bell rings above her head.

The last drop of lukewarm coffee trickles down Emma's throat
as she stares through the glass at the torrential rain outside. She
wonders if it will ever stop. At least she is no longer hungry. Being
as famished as she was, a cardboard cheeseburger and fries tasted
as good as any Steak Diane.

The restaurant is filling up with people younger than she's seen
so far today, many dressed for a night out rather than a day shopping. A couple in their late teens sit on the table directly behind her
and she senses them kissing and cuddling between giggles. Emma
tells herself she is not going to be embarrassed if they are.

Once again, she gazes at the crumpled sheet of paper that she'd rescued from the bin the previous morning. If only Tina had come to her room first instead of delivering refreshments in the usual order, but, of course, the trolley girl wouldn't have known Emma was going to be discharged that morning.

The squiggly lines and random letters that fill the creased sheet are made to look even more nonsensical by the red circles in random places, and a purple asterisk with a strange crescent shape. But they obviously mean something or they wouldn't be on here, Emma reminds herself. She reads aloud some of the initials in the hope their sound will make more sense. NHC, CC, SC, DMC. It is like the hardest of cryptic puzzles. If only she wasn't so tired. Her eyes feel surprisingly heavy for early evening but it has been a particularly exertive first day out of hospital. Perhaps if she rests them for a few minutes.

Still unsure whether she made the right decision her mind fills with images of David Sims and Detective Carr arguing outside the hospital entrance. Until this moment she hasn't given a thought to why the detective finally decided to arrest her. Had he merely been waiting for her to be discharged? If so, he didn't wait long as she had barely stepped outside the hospital door. Maybe that was intentional given David's reluctance to allow her to be questioned. If he had got her home, he may have pulled every string to keep her there.

Then she remembers the so-called photograph, the one which allegedly shows two women getting into a boat. Carr suggested that he was waiting for proof that she was one of those women.

And what if she was? That would mean she may have killed the other woman, whoever that was, and left her to rot in a boat. She clenches her teeth together in frustration. Why is everything about water? Water. That's it! Opening her eyes again she picks up the sheet of paper and sees it in a different way. Of course, the squiggly lines are canals. That means the initials, which all end with C, are the names of canals. And the asterisk and crescent shape show where Dan is. The crescent shape. Yes, now it is obvious.

The strange sensation running through her body must be excitement and it gives her a new lease of energy. She puts on her coat and reaches down for her bag, eager to begin the next stage of her journey. Unable to locate it, she stretches her arm under the seat but can only feel the cold floor tiles. She stands up to take a proper look, and that's when her heart begins to thump in dread. Already realising the terrible truth she bends her head under the plastic chairs and tables to see nothing but crumpled serviettes and a few dropped French fries.

Rushing over to the counter she pushes her way to the front. 'Has anyone handed in my bag?' she shouts to the bored-looking teenager on the till who only shrugs his shoulders.

'Hey!' She grabs the arm of a similar-aged girl on the next till. 'My bag is missing. I'm worried it's been stolen.'

The young girl disappears behind a screen returning with a young man who comes through a gap in the counter and asks Emma to show him where she was sitting.

'Where was your bag, Madam?' he asks sympathetically.

She points to the floor. 'There by my feet. It's a blue leather handbag, and expensive.'

'Did you see anyone close enough to take your bag?'

'No. Nobody came near me while I was here. Wait, there was a couple on the table behind. Maybe they noticed something.' She follows the young man's gaze to the next table. The young couple have gone, and their table is empty of any paper cups or wrappings. 'Oh no. Do you think they could have …?' Of course they did.

'Sit down, Madam. I'll get you a hot drink and we'll call the police. We have security cameras so we should be able to see who took your bag.' He walks away shaking his head.

Emma slumps down on the same plastic chair she's already sat in for over an hour, her mind empty of all thought. At least twenty minutes must have passed before the supervisor appears again with two milky teas, several sachets of sugar and an A5 notepad.

'The police may be a while so they asked me to take some details. What was in the bag?'

'Three hundred pounds,' she replies. He glances up. 'In cash?' She gives a slightly confused nod.

'Any cards?'

'Um yes, one.'

'Just one card,' he says to himself. 'Which card was it?'

'What do you mean?'

He looks up again. 'Which bank issued the card?'

'Oh!' Emma tries to picture the card that is still on the hotel reception desk. She can't. 'Barclays.' It is the first name that comes to mind.

'Okay. You'll need to contact them as soon as possible to cancel the card.'

'Phone?'

She stares at him waiting for further explanation then quickly realises what he means. 'No. I don't have a phone.'

Now he stares at her with his mouth open before continuing. 'Can you describe your bag?'

'Yes. It is dark blue leather with gold clasps.'

'Was it expensive?'

Was it? Probably. 'Yes, but I don't know how much it cost because it was a present.'

'Designer?'

'Um yes, I think so.'

Another look. 'Which designer?'

Despite the good intentions of the young supervisor, his questions are only adding to the misery and making Emma feel like the criminal. What will she say when he asks for her name, address and telephone number? She knows that her bag and, more importantly, the money has gone forever. There is nothing to be gained by wasting any more time. Rather things could get much worse if the police finally arrive. She needs to make yet another escape.

'Could you tell me where the toilets are?' she says shakily.

'I've nearly finished,' he says quickly.

'I really need to go,' she says, standing up and moving back from the table.

He sighs and puts down his pen. 'Upstairs and turn left at the top.'

'Thanks. I'll be back in a few minutes.'

When Emma reaches the stairs, she walks straight past and out of the automatic doors. Then she runs as fast as the driving rain will allow.

CHAPTER FIFTEEN

She's standing on the pavement looking across the road through the rush of cars. Dan's building is in view, its grand façade covering a world of crime. She is frozen to the spot, her eyes fixed on the downstairs window. Beyond the thick glass, a middle-aged woman is barely visible. Emma watches as the worker types her day away without lifting her eyes from some hidden point. She wishes they could swap places, but it is too late now. Blurred images pass behind the woman in the window, and Emma squints in order to refocus her eyes. Dan steps outside and she knows her heart is jumping even though she cannot feel it. She cannot feel anything. Now she is trailing him, and she wonders how they are on the same side. She doesn't remember crossing the busy road. But that isn't important so she keeps walking. He is unaware of her presence behind him, or if he is, doesn't acknowledge her. The distance between them shortens and she is at his shoulder. He smiles and waves but not at her. A woman appears in front of him, and they hug. She is tall, slim and beautiful like a film star. It is her mother.

***

The bus driver takes his time, ignoring the huddle of freezing men and women desperate to escape the damp midnight air. At last the doors spring open and, one by one, the waiting passengers step into the relative warmth of the late-night coach to Bristol. Emma places herself near the back and breathes a sigh of relief when the doors close and the vehicle finally moves off. Holding out for the last bus had not been a difficult decision despite having to wait over three hours for it because, at only fifteen pounds, it was half the price of the earlier one. She keeps her fingers in her pocket and firmly around the remainder of her money - thirty-five pounds. It won't get her much further, but she'll keep going until the bitter end.

Gazing through the rain-splattered window pane she wishes the thieves had at least left her bag behind so it could act as a pillow for her swimming head. Right now she could be lying in a comfortable bed wrapped in a goose-feather quilt, with or without David Sims. On the other hand, she could be lying on a wooden board in a police cell. She closes her eyes and visualises Detective Carr. Considering she has only met him briefly, his image is clear and almost tangible. He is standing at the foot of her hospital bed writing in that tiny notebook. Then, after placing it in his pocket, he walks over and takes her in his arms. A warm sensation flows through her body but disappears when her head hits the seat in front, waking her up. Why couldn't he be the man who wants to save her? What she would give for that dream to become a reality.

As the bus pulls away from the city, its wheels shift into a regular motion and the atmosphere onboard becomes more and more relaxing. Emma lifts up the large collar of her coat and, using it as a makeshift pillow, drifts back into a fitful sleep. But this time it is not the handsome detective who is present in her deep consciousness.

The traffic is unusually heavy as Emma and her friend step off the bus and join the early morning shoppers. It is hardly Oxford Street, but the nearest town high street will have to do for an anniversary present. Rosa has taken some persuading as the trip means missing her mid-morning run, something that Emma doesn't fully understand. It isn't just that she doesn't get the appeal of running long distances to lose weight that you don't have in the first place. If Rosa wants to run, why can't she run when they get back? The shopping trip will only take a couple of hours at the most. But the new Rosa likes her routine despite having no regular job or fixed abode since taking a sabbatical from acting and renting an old beach hut on a weekly basis. Emma knows it's selfish but she's happy having her friend around again. Who else could she moan to about Dan? And it gives her a chance to make up for neglecting their friendship these past few years.

As they walk past a Georgian building standing alone amongst the nineteen-sixties concrete blocks, Emma holds her breath. It belongs to Dan's legal firm, and she hasn't told him about meeting

up with Rosa. If he spots them through the window, he'll be sure
to sulk for the next few days. But apart from a solitary woman
sitting behind a typewriter, there is no sign of life through the front
windows. Emma supposes the solicitors are all hidden in the back
offices in case a client wanders in unexpectedly and takes a minute
of their unpaid time. She thinks of the poor secretary sitting alone
all day with nothing to keep her company except the postman and
the odd enquirer. Hopefully, she has a family home filled with love
and laughter to make up for the Dickensian workplace.

The two young women drift in and out of shop after shop,
together yet miles apart. Rosa expresses a positive opinion of every
single item Emma shows her then looks irritated when the item is
ruled out. She is clearly bored, and Emma feels under pressure to
buy something sooner rather than later. A girlie retail therapy trip
it most certainly is not, yet Emma insists on delaying its end a while
longer.

'Do you think it's tacky buying them matching presents?' she
asks, staring at the two watches lying in identical gift boxes.

'How could anything be tacky at that price?' Rosa replies, sip-
ping her black coffee. 'Anyway, people always hate their presents so
it wouldn't matter what you got them. They'll just be placed in a
drawer to gather dust and never see the light of day again.'

'Well, thanks for that. I've just spent a fortune on these stupid
watches. Perhaps we should go back to the jewellers.' She notices
her friend's shoulders slump and adds quickly, 'Then again, it was
Dan who said to give a lot. You know how he worships my dad.'

A frosty atmosphere descends and Emma knows it is at the mention of her fiancé. Rosa is no more a fan of Dan than he is of her. Up until now, Emma has avoided mentioning him but something is on her mind. She decides to reach out to the Rosa she used to know.

'Rosa, I think Dan might be having an affair.'

She looks up, her dark blue eyes seeming even larger than usual. 'You're not married, Em.' Then her tone changes slightly. 'What makes you say that though?'

Emma doesn't react to her friend's belittling comment. 'While I was putting away the laundry, something fell from the top shelf of the airing cupboard. It was a packet of condoms. I'm on the pill.'

A longer gap in conversation follows, and the din of the fast-food restaurant descends between the two friends. Rosa continues gnawing at her food and Emma watches as a skinny chip gradually disappears between two red fingernails and matching lips which somehow manage to curl upwards.

'It's not funny, Rosa.'

'What do you mean? I haven't even said anything, Em.'

'No, but you grinned. Why did I even tell you? Dan always said you wanted to split us up?'

Now Rosa frowns. 'Hang on! So, I'm the villain now, am I? It's not my fault if he's doing the dirty on you.'

'We don't know that for definite. There could be another explanation. I was hoping you could help me think of one.'

'Like what? He's got a sexually transmitted disease. Either way, Em, someone's been playing around.' Instead of showing sadness,

Rosa's eyes are glistening like the ocean on a clear night. There is no sympathy no support, no friendship.

The bus shudders to a halt, and Emma opens her eyes to her own reflection. It is still dark outside. An hour to wait until the connection, and it should be starting to get light by the time she arrives. That's just as well as she will have to rely on the direction of strangers for the last leg of this journey. But it is a world full of strangers. Even Dan belongs to the unknown.

As Emma surveys each colourful vessel, she marvels at the tranquillity of canal life. It is a far cry from twenty-first, even twentieth-century existence. It's a world in which she imagines nothing has changed for many years. For centuries. The idyllic scenery, the gentle sway of the water, the rhythmic humming of the engine. Emma tries to picture this faraway scene before accepting it would be unrealistic. There would have been nothing romantic about the coal-filled barges being dragged through the stinking polluted water by overworked horses. Or families cramped into rotting boats because they could never afford to live on land. She should stop viewing the past through rose-tinted spectacles.

Without warning a loud bang brings these private musings inside her head to an abrupt end, and a man's head pops out of a green wooden cuboid twenty feet ahead. Her heart almost leaps out of her mouth when she sees him.

Daniel Merriman jumps onto the canal path with the ease of any twenty-year-old. Leaning his long body over the ropes, he laughs at something a pretty young woman in the neighbouring barge has said. Jealousy surges through Emma, and she realises her feelings for him are not playing along with any pretence of moving on. Sensing the daggers boring into her, the young woman instinctively raises her head slightly which is enough to cause Dan to look behind him. His eyes squint in the sun until his smile drops.

Their eyes lock, the world stands still and everything and everyone else disappears from view. There are just the two of them. Music swirls around Emma's head as she is back in her parent's sitting room, her last clear memory of her previous life. He is watching her as she sways against the other dancers, younger guests at the middle-aged people's party. Someone is smoking dope, and the fumes are playing with her head. A hand presses a joint between her fingers. Just as she is about to take a drag, he rushes forward and kisses her passionately. She is in heaven.

'How did you find me?'

She opens her eyes and looks through the dissipating smoke. Dan is standing in front of her but his eyes are cold, serving as barriers against the unwelcome presence approaching him. After a moment that seems like an age, she finally summons up the strength to speak.

'You know I always wanted to be a detective,' she says, forcing a smile that he doesn't return. 'Would you believe I found you on a computer screen? You always told me that technology would eventually reveal our location wherever we were in this world.'

'That wasn't me.'

The rebuttal throws her, and she fumbles about with silent words while trying to respond. He doesn't wait.

'What do you want?' The tone is as harsh as his eyes.

Emma is painfully aware that she is not welcome on this canal path. To make matters worse, the surroundings are beginning to force their way through the trance she's been in. The woman in the barge is staring at her, curiosity expressed in her creased-up face. Emma is now self-conscious besides being lost for words. Why didn't she rehearse for the situation she has put herself in? Nerves are beginning to overwhelm her, and she wants to reverse away from this hostile audience of two. The only other option is to keep calm and carry on, but she cannot think of anything useful to say. Surprisingly, she is rescued by her former boyfriend.

'You look terrible. Are you ill?'

'Well, thanks for that. You're looking a bit weathered, too, Dan,' she says.

His face crumples with irritation. 'Sorry for showing concern. If you've come here to make silly remarks, I've got better things to do.' He shakes his head as if reprimanding a naughty child.

You know I always make stupid jokes when I'm nervous, Emma wants to say. It is the first time she has been in Dan's company for months, decades even. She has allowed her twenty-three-year-old head to come to the fore. Pushing it into the background is particularly difficult this time. 'I...er...I need to talk to you. I need you to answer some questions for me.' In spite of the dozens of words crashing around inside her head, this is all she manages to express.

'Questions? Now?'

'I'm sorry if you're busy. Maybe some other time?'

'Yes, I am busy, but that's not what I meant. Why now after all these years?'

Because nothing makes sense, she screams inside her head. 'Things have happened since then, Dan. I need you to help me understand them.'

'It's called life. Life happens, and sometimes it's shit. For some, it's shittier than others. What is there to understand?'

'So much, Dan. There is so much I need help understanding. And you're the only person who can do that.' It must have sounded ridiculous, not to mention self- indulgent and she thinks he is going to walk away. But then he holds a lean arm out towards his barge. 'I assume you want privacy. You'd better come inside.'

Chapter Sixteen

Darkness surrounds them. His skin is soft and warm. His lips are hungry. Passion overcomes her senses, and she doesn't know where she is. Only that she is with him. There is no moon to expose their nakedness, no luminous planets to catch their shimmering skin. Her limbs stretch out as he moves around her body. He bends forward and she kisses the top of his head. Now she can feel the ground beneath them. It is soft like unmown grass. They are outside, probably in a garden, someone's garden. It is so daring it adds to the excitement. The moment comes and she cries though no sound emits from her open mouth. He lifts his head from her neck and kisses her one last time. She opens her eyes but he is gone, and she is lying alone. Something, a sound, a movement, a feeling, makes her turn her head. A figure is standing by a tree, too far away to identify, but close enough for her to know it is a woman. The moon emerges from behind the clouds and shines down on her naked body. She is filled with shame.

***

After tottering across a warped plank of wood, Emma finds herself standing on the home of her ex-fiancé. The last time they were together she could have leapt from one surface to the other with no fear of falling in. But now is not the time to dwell on such things. Her time with Dan will be limited, and she needs to stay focussed on her objective.

He has disappeared through a hole in the side of the barge, and with much trepidation, she follows him. She crouches down as she enters the living quarters all the time reminding herself that they are not underwater. It just feels like it. The space inside is tiny, and she wonders where the bed is before realising that she might be sitting on it. With barely enough room to move without touching each other, he remains standing which adds to his unwelcoming demeanour. He waits in silence for her to speak first.

'Dan, it's been so long since I saw you last. Why is that?' Emma cringes as soon as the words leave her mouth. The question is more suitable for an old work colleague rather than the man she once loved. And this is not lost on Dan.

'You know perfectly well. Why are you even asking me that?' He shakes his head in apparent disbelief.

'Because I don't remember. Really, I don't.' It is too late for Emma to start again so she no longer cares about the wisdom of her questions. 'You know, Dan, since the accident my past life is a blur. It's like I'm -'

'What accident?'

'Oh you don't know, do you? I've just been released from hospital after nearly drowning. I was in a coma for a while and when I woke up I didn't know anything, not even who I was, then, then ...' She needs to take a breath to build up to the next part.

He is staring at her, his expression unsympathetic. 'What's this got to do with me? Surely you should be asking other people to help you with this. I have no idea what's been going on in your life.'

'But you are the only person who can help me, Dan. I'm not only talking about the past few years but back when we were ... living together.' She lowers her eyes afraid to look at his face.

'I think you should leave. There's nothing I can do for you, and I need to get on.' The hostility in his voice remains.

Before answering, Emma pauses to think. She has to be careful what she says to this man who is acting like a stranger. He is no longer the lovestruck fiancé who would do anything for her, and she couldn't talk to him as if he were. 'This is going to sound crazy, but I can't remember anything about my life since the night of my parents' party.' She waits for a reaction. There is none so she continues. 'I don't know what happened to Rosa. Nor anything about my parents getting ill. Not even you. The last time I remember us being together, we were engaged. In love. I accept all that's gone. But instead of memories, there is a dark chasm between then and now.'

Dan sighs. 'Do you honestly expect people to believe that?'

'No, of course not. But it's the truth, I swear. I accept that I went through it, and it really happened, and that I remembered it once.

But it's gone, knocked out by the boat fall maybe, but it's no longer there.'

'Then you need to see a doctor, not me. How am I supposed to help you? I couldn't ...' He trails off before finishing.

'The doctors say things will return in time. But I can't wait for that to happen. I don't even remember Rosa dying yet I've discovered I was arrested and charged with her murder.'

His cheeks burn up at this direction of conversation. He juts out his jaw as he breathes out slowly. 'Why are you bringing this up again?'

'Just tell me what happened, please. Tell me what I did. Because I swear to you, I don't remember.'

He looks at her incredulously, his mouth open. She winces as she waits for the inevitable onslaught of verbal abuse, the next accusation of lying, the showing of the door. But there is something about his expression, something familiar, that changes the dread to apprehension. What is he going to say? She holds her breath.

'That's what you said at the time.'

She stands up so she can face him. 'I know I did but tell me anyway. What did I do to Rosa?' There is a long silence, and she wants to shake him just like she wanted to shake Mrs Weekes and Tina.

At last, he relents. 'Okay. I'll play along. Somebody pushed her off the cliff and she drowned. First, they said it was you, then they let you go. There is nothing more to say.'

'Did anyone see me do it? There must have been witnesses or, surely, I wouldn't have been charged.'

He shakes his head. 'Not exactly. A man passing on his fishing boat saw two people tussling on the cliff top then one being pushed off.'

'Two people. But he couldn't tell who they were. Rosa was obviously one person, and they assumed I was the other. Why? How come I was charged? It makes no sense. Why did they think I was coldblooded enough to kill my best friend?'

'Because a short time earlier you'd threatened to kill your best friend in front of everyone at the party. That's why they knew it was you. There was nobody else with a motive.'

'But that's just a turn of phrase. I've said it to you enough times. And how could they *know* it was me when it *wasn't*? The charges against me were dropped, Dan.'

'Okay. They thought it was you.'

'So, what was my motive? What were we arguing about?'

He pauses before continuing. 'You accused me and Rosa of sleeping together.' Despite the biting tone of his instant reply, his pink cheeks betray his embarrassment.

Images flash in front of her. Dreams of the people in her younger life. Rosa. Dan. Arguing. Crying. Dreams or memories? 'And were you?' she says, matching his coldness.

'Emma, what difference would it make now? It's all in the past and nothing could change what happened.' It is the first time he's said her name.

'It matters to me, Dan,' she says, her voice now quaking. 'We were so happy. We were going to marry, spend our lives together. Did Rosa ruin everything for us?'

His voice remains dispassionate. 'Of course, she ruined every-thing. She was jealous and destructive. I told you over and over again, but you wouldn't listen.'

Hearing the vitriol in Dan's voice, Emma is surprised he wasn't accused of Rosa's murder himself. And why hasn't he answered her question? 'Well you know what they say – it takes two to tango.'

His eyes narrow. 'What's that supposed to mean?'

She swallows hard before speaking. 'I found a packet of con-doms in our airing cupboard. You must have been using them for someone, Dan. Were they for Rosa?'

'Get out of here.'

If only she could take the words back, but it is too late now. All she can do is try to salvage the situation or at least get some sort of confession. After all, her point is a valid one. 'Okay. I'll go but why can't you just tell me the truth? Like you said, what difference would it make now other than to give me some closure.'

'I never slept with Rosa. In fact, I used to do as much as I could to avoid being in the same space as her.'

Placing one hand on her chest Emma breathes a sigh of relief. As irrelevant as it now is, the thought of her best friend and her fiancé together is incredibly painful to her. But it is immediately replaced by a more disturbing one. If not Rosa, then who? The dream of her mother with Dan replays in her mind. Was her mother's dislike of him nothing more than a cover? Emma cannot leave at this juncture but needs to distract herself from the latest crazy thought.

'How did I end up in hospital?'

Perhaps taken aback by Emma returning to the earlier point in the conversation, Dan seems to have forgotten his own demand for her to leave. 'You took a boat out to sea either to finish Rosa off or kill yourself.'

'I climbed down from the clifftop?'

'No. You made your way down to the bay and then rowed out. I suppose that shows you didn't actually want to die.'

'How do you work that out?'

He rolls his eyes. 'Because you would have jumped off the clifftop too.'

'But apparently, I did almost die.'

'No one knew what your intentions were going out there like that, but the boat capsized throwing you into the water too. You were in a coma for a week after that and, when you woke up, you said you remembered nothing about the night. I see you still haven't recovered. Why don't you come back in another thirty years, and we'll do this all over again? And on that note ... '

But his words are drowned out by the engine of a passing barge. Before he can repeat them, a female voice calls through the open hatch and Dan climbs outside leaving Emma alone. It is obvious that he was about to tell her to go again, and she is not sure she is physically or mentally able to delay the inevitable for a second or third time. From outside muffled voices enter the narrow dingy space via the same gap Dan left minutes before. One is female and another pang of jealousy hits Emma in the heart. This is proving far more painful than she expected. Suddenly the urge to leave takes over the desire for answers. Getting to her feet too quickly she stumbles against the opposite wall finding herself falling to the floor. It is too much, and she feels tears forming in her sore eyes.

'What happened?' Dan is standing over her holding a plastic cup in one hand and a bread roll in the other. He makes no effort to help her up.

'Oh, nothing.' She straightens herself. 'I'll leave you to your breakfast. Thanks for sparing me some time.' As she brushes herself down, her body sways to the side once again, so she sits back on the hard board. 'If I could just have a minute.'

'Here. You look like you need these more than I do,' he says, holding out the drink and bacon bap.

Emma's eyes prick with tears at this first display of kindness but also the latest reminder that the bond between them has long since died. It seems like only weeks ago that they would have happily shared the breakfast. 'Could you just pour me some in a cup? My mouth is really dry so I don't want anything to eat.'

After he hands her the half-filled plastic cup, Emma cherishes the warm milky drink that moistens her mouth. 'When did you start drinking tea?' she asks, immediately regretting the personal question.

But Dan doesn't answer it. Instead, he sits on a stool and drinks back his tea in a few gulps. 'Look I've genuinely got to make a move now. Where are you going when you leave here?'

It takes her by surprise, and she doesn't know how to respond. Does she even know herself? It took her two hours to get from the train station to the marina so that's another two hours back. And then where? 'I don't know, Dan. I'm on the run.'

His expression doesn't change. 'From him?'

'From everyone.'

He stands up, puts down his cup and walks up the steps into the morning air leaving Emma alone in the barge. She stares across at the bacon roll wondering why he didn't eat it. Perhaps he's left it for her but she is not hungry, only tired. She closes her burning eyes leaving her other senses to absorb the surroundings. Beneath her, the seat is hard and narrow suggesting that it does not double up as a bed, or at least is not the main sleeping area. Even so, she could quite easily unfold her cold and aching limbs on it in the unlikely event Dan should make the offer. Time passes and the only sounds are unrecognisable. Then she realises the barge is moving.

The way ahead is breathtaking, almost too perfect to be real. Gone is the narrow and fairly murky canal they'd been floating on earlier. Instead is a wide expanse of water glistening with the reflection of huge weeping willows against a deep blue sky. There is not a house or person in sight. A gaggle of Canada geese swim alongside adding to the picture postcard scene, though spoiling the tranquillity with their honking and hissing. At least it drowns out the sound of the diesel engine.

Emma sits on the bow of the narrowboat and soaks up the experience she never expected to have. When she first emerged from inside the boat, fuzzy-headed and blurry-eyed from a deep sleep, she panicked assuming that Dan had fallen overboard leaving her hopelessly adrift. Then she noticed his face staring at her from the bottom end of the boat. No, he wasn't staring at her at all, but rather into the distance. Yet another person in complete control of her immediate future. Eventually, the narrowboat eases over to the bank and Dan shuffles his way back to the front. As soon as he jumps off to secure the barge, they hear the sound of an invisible train passing. 'This part of the canal runs alongside a train route. We'll be at the stop in an hour.'

Emma nods. 'Thanks. I was dreading the walk back.' She has no idea which train station they are heading to.

'Come on. Time for a drink.' He holds out his hand.

The pub, nestled between the canal and a vast forest, is seemingly inaccessible other than by boat, and Emma wonders if the owners actually need any customers. Yet inside it is filled to the rafters with loud and high-spirited punters, clearly a hub for like-minded drifters. And for Emma, it is a chance to use the bathroom while holding onto a crumb of dignity. She and Dan may have lived in each other's pockets once, but that was then and this is now. Unfortunately, the reflection in the mirror is the latter. It is a sight she still isn't used to seeing: the shadows under her eyes, the strands of grey, and the lines around her mouth. She barely recognises the image apart from what she can see of her mother's features. But the reflection no longer makes her jump.

Dan is at the bar chatting and laughing with the barman. Standing awkwardly behind him, she considers it a side to him she has never seen before: friendly, jovial, and relaxed; perhaps the solitary canal life suits him better than she did. At last, he turns around handing her a glass of red wine and nodding towards a tiny table near the door. She sits on one of the two hardwood chairs facing each other before taking a big swig from the glass. It is a much stronger wine than she is used to, and she begins coughing fearing she will be sick. When she eventually composes herself, she says, 'It went down the wrong way.'

He looks at the coat she's yet to take off and says, 'You got a bit on your collar. They'll get that out for you at the bar.'

'Oh it doesn't bother me,' she says, wondering why he thought it would in the current context.

'It looks expensive,' he says. 'I suppose if you have more at home ...'

'I'm not going home, Dan, at least not until I have no choice in the matter.'

He takes a sip of his beer, wipes the froth from his lips and upper beard, and then leans forward. 'Tell me again why you've left him.'

There is a long pause while Emma considers what she should say in response to Dan's command. She hasn't actually told him anything about her experience in hospital because she's been too wrapped up in their past relationship. What would he do if she told him she's been arrested for murder yet again? But there is no other option.

'Dan, I haven't actually left him.'

So, she tells him the whole story from waking up in hospital to the point of running away. It is surprising how little time it takes to relay the details, perhaps because she focuses more on the detective than David whom she sees as secondary in importance. 'And that's about it. Apparently, your former fiancée is a serial killer.'

At this moment two men turn around and glance down at her before restarting their own private conversation. The action is brief but it is one that reminds Emma she is not in her own private space with Dan, able to be as crazy as she was in her hospital room.

But even if Dan noticed the two men, it hasn't bothered him. 'Who is this second woman? You haven't said anything about her.'

This time Emma lowers her voice. 'Because I don't know anything about her, Dan. Not even her name.'

'And you haven't seen a photograph of her or a newspaper clipping?'

She shakes her head. 'I just have to take his word for it that she exists, existed. Like you have to take my word for it that the detective exists.'

Dan's expression remains fixed and inscrutable even while taking a phone from his pocket and tapping away at it in silence. Finally, he says, 'There's no report of a woman found dead at sea. What that means regarding your detective, I have no idea.' He puts his phone back in his pocket.

Emma is frozen to the spot. Around her, the raucous laughter and clinking of glasses fade into silence, and all she can hear are the words of Dan's first sentence on a loop inside her head - *no report of a woman found dead*. At last, she is able to respond to his question, at least in her mind. So what? How would you even know that from your phone? Hundreds of women die every day. But then she remembers what David said about knowing everything. And of course, Tina's brother.

'Emma, did you hear what I said?'

She nods. 'Yes, but like you, I don't know what that means. The detective must exist because Dav ... '

He takes another swig of his beer. 'What about David? It's okay to say his name. I have moved on.'

But I haven't, she thinks. 'David spoke to him at least twice. He tried to stop him arresting me which was why I had a chance to escape.' She cringes at the choice of words. 'I guess that makes me sound guilty but I was just scared, Dan. That's why I looked for you. All I wanted was to be with you again.'

'Two savoury pies.'

A slight gamey aroma hits Emma's nostrils as she views the plate which has just been placed in front of her. Looking across the table she can see Dan is already devoting his attention to the pie. Her stomach turns, yet she is crying out for food at the same time so she picks up the knife and fork.

'There's nothing here for you, Emma. It's time to go back.'

'I know. There's just one more place I need to go first.'

'Well, I've taken you as close as I can. The train is due in another thirty minutes.'

'Oh. Have I got time to finish this?'

'Finish what?'

'The pie.'

'What pie?'

Dan is still facing her but he is standing in the doorway of the barge. There is no pub. She gets up and follows him out of the barge and onto the canal path.

CHAPTER SEVENTEEN

The family is complete. Father, mother and daughter are together at last. They are sitting around an oval table but the distance between them is not equal. She is alone in her half. An oversized silver candelabra is blocking the view of her parents and she wants to remove it. But it is too heavy, and she cannot lift it. There is nothing else on the table. No plates, no bottles, no cutlery. She wonders who is going to bring in the food. Will there be any? The air around them is cold and she wishes she wasn't sitting in her nightdress. She notices the candelabra is no longer there, and she can see all around her. When she looks across the table, her mother is shivering too. But her father seems hot and bothered. He takes off his jumper and sits half-naked. Emma is embarrassed and begins to cry. Her mother tells her to stop being silly as she is no longer a child. Then the table grows in size and her mother and father are getting further and further away from her. She waves at them, but they look straight through her before vanishing.

***

The train stop, because it is a stop not a station, is the most isolated place Emma has been. Concrete steps lead down to a narrow, deserted platform with a solitary stone bench. The single track stretches about one hundred yards each way before curving out of sight, resembling those many images of paths into the afterlife. She could end up going either way but the choice will not be hers. It will depend on the direction of the first train that arrives. And she must get on it as Dan will be wanting to go back to his barge.

The sun has made a rare unblemished appearance in the sky bringing with it a welcome warmth to the late autumn air, yet a chilly atmosphere remains around the man and woman sitting on opposite sides of the stone bench. They both sit in silence waiting for the first sign of the train. Anyone watching would assume they are a long-married couple, content if slightly bored with one another's company. But there is no one else there, and the train is taking a long time.

Emma pulls out the money from her coat pocket and counts it for the umpteenth time. Thirty-five pounds. No more, no less. It should get her back to London if she manages to reach a town with a bus station. This sudden movement causes her detached companion to turn his head, and she takes the chance to break the silence.

'What happened to us, Dan? We were so in love. Why are we both talking to each other as strangers, not as husband and wife?'

His eyes are now fixed back on the rusted steel rails. 'Because you didn't love me enough, Emma.'

She is taken aback at the accusation. 'Dan, why would you even say that?'

'Because it's the truth. When you came out of hospital, you married the lawyer that hadn't been sacked, the lawyer who got the promotion. You deserted me.'

'Sacked? Hang on. Do you mean David got the promotion instead of you? But why? It was all in the bag for you, Dan. You were going to be a partner.'

'Because I coached your father with his alibi. Someone overheard us on the office phone and recorded the conversation. The partners said they would not go to the police if I left quietly. I had little choice.'

Her heart is pounding. 'Who taped the conversation?' He shrugs.

'I don't know, and it doesn't matter.'

'It matters to me, Dan. Was it David?'

'Just because he benefitted from my sacking, it doesn't mean he was responsible for it. It could have been anyone who was working there that day.'

Emma pictures the secretary sitting alone at her desk. Was it her or David? She is not sure it should matter to her anyway. 'And you risked all that for me. How could I have left you? We were going to get married.' Then she remembers something David said. 'Are you sure it wasn't the other way around? Maybe it was you who gave up on me.'

His eyes are now filled with pain. 'I would have done anything for you then, even died for you. As you said, we were supposed to spend the rest of our lives together, but we didn't and that's that.'

They continue to sit in silence, she, absorbing the shocking details of their split for the first time, he, reliving them. Suddenly the past thirty years disintegrate and the hurt and betrayal are unbearable. How could she abandon him when she'd loved him so much, when he had put everything on the line for her? It is too horrible to comprehend. What sort of person has she become? The guilt is more painful than anything she's experienced since waking up in the hospital, even the shock of ageing. She can't face him any longer. It seems he feels the same way.

'I need to move on, Emma,' he says, as the sound of a horn is heard.

'I know.' She stands up and stares at the train getting nearer and closer and finally stopping in front of them.

She steps into the empty carriage, and he shuts the door behind her, nudging her arm to ensure she is inside. It is the last time he will touch her. There are no words left. She sits down on the seat furthest from the door and sobs.

The taxi driver gives her an odd look as she asks how much the fare to Pickford would be. When he says thirty pounds, she jumps in the car without asking if he will take the fare even though it is more than she'd hoped. She's got too far now to quibble over a few pounds. For a while, the train had taken her alongside the canal, moving further away from Dan with every rotation of the wheel. Eventually, it turned towards the setting sun, and, after thirty minutes or so, the scenery began to look familiar. Her heart almost exploded when she realised where she was heading. Home. Her real home. And for once something else was going her way. No conductor came around to check her ticket, so she has held on to her meagre funds. Until now. The driver accepts the fare but insists on payment first.

'Now let's see if I can find my way to this house,' he says to himself, as he climbs back into the car and starts the engine before taking the loneliest exit off a roundabout.

Emma bites her tongue. If she were the one driving, they would go straight to her parents' old house with no chance of getting lost. At least that is how it feels. It seems like only weeks since she was there talking and laughing with her mother and father. Hugging them. She digs her nails into her palms to keep the tears at bay.

'Well this is the last turning,' he says, slowing the car down to a crawl. 'Sycamore Drive. I'll have to do a three-point turn if this isn't it. Then we're back to square one.'

Sycamore Drive. They are almost there. 'Take the turning. It's at the end of this road.'

It isn't a road as such but more of a track. The driver groans as his expensive tyres trundle over potholes, ditches and ridges. The road is much worse than Emma remembers, another sign of the many years that have passed between visits. A white building appears on the left which Emma immediately recognises as belonging to Mrs Weekes. She waits for the taxi driver to comment but he is focused on saving his wheel axils and cursing under his breath.

As they drive by slowly, Emma peers through each gap in the hedgerow, looking for signs of life – parked cars, washing, a dog bowl or even Mrs Weekes. To her bitter disappointment, there are none. Telling herself it doesn't matter, she turns her attention to the house that lies ahead. A feeling of dread rises inside her as if she knows they are driving towards something terrible. As they approach the end of the lane, she can see the wrought iron weathervane which her mother hated. A voice inside her is shouting STOP! GO BACK. TURN AROUND. YOU CAN'T DEAL WITH THIS.

But now they've arrived at the gate. She steps out of the car and holds her hands to her face.

White Hills stands proudly in its solitude. Despite its classic style, the elegant building could have been built two months rather than two hundred years ago. The beautiful Georgian windows glisten in their princely white casements; the casements that were always slightly open whatever the weather outside. They are open now. In the centre of the house, completing the perfect symmetrical design, is a sage green oak panelled door. The same door. It is as if nothing has changed. Emma soaks up every detail unperturbed at the fact that the taxi, having done a rapid three-point turn, is now driving away. But it doesn't matter because she is here at last. The gate is open, and she walks into the huge driveway.

There is little point in closing the gate behind her as it is rare that unwelcome or uninvited visitors come this far down the lane. She stands on the path and listens to the music coming from inside the house. Someone is playing the piano. She tries to identify the poignant notes filtering through one of the open windows. The tune is so familiar. It sounds like Schubert, her father's favourite. It sounds like her father is playing it. He must love that tune so much because she hears it so often these days.

The piano playing stops and a curtain moves in his music room. His head appears at the window. He smiles and waves. She can see he is still wearing that baggy grey jumper. Emma laughs. Things are as they always were. He is inside the house. He never left. She is young again. Everything is going to be all right. She can hear her mother calling her, her voice getting louder and louder. Tears of relief stream down her face as the moment overwhelms her.

'Hello!'

Now the window is open wider, and her mother's head is visible behind the dark frames. Dark frames? It is not their window. It is not her mother. Emma scans the scene in front of her once again. Suddenly the pristine walls are stained with soot and Ivy trailing up to the roof. There is no piano music, no weathervane, no mother, no father.

'I'm so sorry. We're a bit lost.'

Emma spins around to see an embarrassed-looking David standing by the gate. No. There is no gate, just a gap in the hedge.

He walks up to Emma and mutters under his breath, 'I knew this was one of the places you were likely to be.'

At this moment Emma hates him. She hates him for finding her. She hates him for being dishonest and not telling the woman the actual reason she is there. But most of all she hates him for being real, for not being a figment of her imagination just like her mum and dad were seconds earlier. How cruel the mind can be.

'Oh. Where are you going?' the woman says, now poking her head further out of the window.

'Er, Mrs Weekes' house. We heard she was unwell and wanted to check if she got home okay.' By now he has his arm around Emma's waist.

The woman closes the window and then, a few seconds later, opens the door. She is shaking her head. 'I'm so sorry but Mrs Weekes passed away a couple of months ago. How did you know she was unwell?'

'My wife was in the same hospital. I'm sorry to hear she passed away.'

The woman is now staring at Emma but continues talking to David. 'To be honest, we didn't know her much. There is a son who looked after her, so we didn't need to call around that often.'

There is an awkward silence as no one knows how to depart from the situation. Finally, David tucks his arm under Emma's and guides her back slightly. 'Well thank you for telling us. We'll be on our way,' he says, before increasing the force of his arm. 'Sorry for disturbing you,' he calls out to the woman, as she disappears behind the brown door.

Disturbing you. Emma is aware of the double meaning of David's apology. The woman had looked quite scared until David, in his reassuring manner, lied about why they were there. Is my appearance so unnerving to strangers? she wonders.

He opens his car door and says, 'Come on Darling. Let's get you home.'

As they trundle back down the lane, Emma looks up at Mrs Weekes' house once more. For the first time, she notices a for sale sign propped against the gate post. The sign is so prominent that she wonders how she missed it on the way down. Perhaps she wasn't looking hard enough. The silence inside the car is broken by the sound of music coming from the radio. This unnecessary noise suggests even David has had quite enough of his wife's crazy behaviour for the time being.

A pang of guilt stabs her conscience as she thinks of Dan on his barge after being robbed of the career he'd loved so much. And now she was going home with the man she abandoned him for, the man who had stolen his promotion as well as his girlfriend. David told her it was the other way around, that it was Dan who deserted her when she was at her sickest. He must have told her that to protect her from the truth – that Dan had done what he did for her. But Dan will never forgive her. She saw it in his eyes.

David is the only one who can help her get through the rest of this life. And so far he's done everything in her interests, even after she'd run away from him when he'd been so supportive and caring. He was going to take care of her and keep away the people who mean her harm. She wasn't ready to listen then, but he was right, just like he's been right about everything. She needs to take his advice from now on. It is time to trust him.

'I don't recall it being so quiet,' David comments, getting out of the car. 'We made the right decision moving away. The kids would have hated it.'

Despite having no memory of "the kids", Emma nods as if in agreement. To her, the place is as she left it however long ago that was. Three decades or three months. So far she's seen nothing to suggest that thirty years have passed by since then. Only trees, pathways, wild birds and the odd car, all timeless in their own way. Even the buildings, sparse as they are, show no sign of the twenty-first century. The one they are about to enter has looked the same for over five hundred years. But inside the grounds, they encounter the first indisputable proof that the year 1993 was a long long time ago.

The headstone is big enough to hold two names but for now holds only one: Jonathan Watt. Emma touches her neck. It won't be long, she knows, until her mother is here too. The tiny plot is a surprise. Emma knows that her parents didn't want to be cremated. She remembers the many conversations she had with both of them, with her making jokes about being buried alive while they insisted it was the proper way. At least you are giving something back to the earth, her father would say, while for her mother it was a matter of religion; cremation might obstruct the resurrection of the soul.

This concept was far beyond the young Emma's comprehension, but she never had to think about it back then. Things are different now. Jennifer Watt is sitting in some nursing home and at the mercy of carers for her basic needs. Emma and David are the only people who can take care of her mother's spiritual wishes. She doubts the younger family members are interested.

Ignoring her aching knees, Emma crouches down and wipes away some of the cobwebs and dust on the granite stone. The motions of a sob break out in her throat but there are no tears left to cry. Somehow it makes the grief more intense. Her father disappeared within the blink of an eye.

One minute a healthy man, the next dead. Why isn't he still alive to help her deal with all this? Lately, she's needed him more than ever before. Even if he were elderly, at least he would be here with her, living in the same time and space.

The date of death still seems futuristic: 17th July 2021, well into the twenty-first century. Why doesn't the date sound familiar to her? It's not as if he's been gone that long. People never forget the anniversary of a loved one's death, do they? She closes her eyes to indulge in her last memory of her father. But as much as she tries, her mind remains blank.

'Do you think my mother had affairs?' she says, as they walk back to the car.

David pulls a face. 'To be honest, the thought has never crossed my mind. What makes you ask?'

'Didn't she start wearing brighter clothes and more makeup for a while?'

'As I remember her, she was always in bright clothes.'

'Not always,' Emma counters. 'Most of my memories are of her wearing lighter colours, fawns and beiges, not bright red. If you don't remember her that way, she must have altered her style about the time we met.'

'I suppose so. You know her far better than I do,' he says, betraying a lack of interest in the subject.

In contrast, Emma is suddenly obsessed. 'Why bother changing in your late forties? She'd spent her whole adult life a picture of elegance and class, yet my last images are of her wearing loud and garish clothes, even to the point of looking tarty.'

'That's not nice,' he says light-heartedly.

'I know it isn't, but I don't want to think of my mother dressed like that. My father would have hated it, I'm sure. He loved her the way she was.'

He is silent for a while before finally responding. 'Perhaps he didn't notice.'

'What do you mean? Of course, he would have noticed. They still loved each other.' But she isn't sure about this statement. Is it just a romantic assumption that children have of their parents' relationship?

'Maybe it was a midlife crisis? It might have been her way of proving to herself she was still attractive. Our late forties are, after all, the last few stops before fifty.'

Emma doesn't react to his tactless remark as she still cannot relate to having reached fifty herself. Instead, she continues along the same path. 'It's hard to imagine my mother worried about age. She always had a timeless quality to her. If she was able to dress herself, I could imagine her wearing the same clothes today.'

He groans. 'Unfortunately, Jennifer isn't able to dress herself so we'll never know what her preference would be if she were.' Then more gently, he says, 'Stop looking for mysteries where there are none to be found. Your mother went through a funny phase that's all.'

'Which has continued right up until now? That must be twenty years or so, David.'

'Maybe, but she always looks good,' he laughs.

'Even once she hit fifty?' Emma cannot resist the barbed comment.

'Hey,' he says, taking her hand in his and kissing it, 'you will always be beautiful to me, Emma.'

She smiles despite not caring for the backhanded compliment. Suddenly the conversation about her mother is making her focus on herself. How does she look to David? Is their relationship one that is no longer passionate? Not that this would be unusual after being together for so many years. But to her battered mind, they are only just getting to know each other. A memory of their first meeting flashes through her mind. David looked like an old man to her then. Yet now she is used to his face, and it is an attractive one. What will happen when they go back to the house he keeps mentioning? It is yet another unknown.

'It's getting late. We need to decide what we're doing. I could ring up that hotel we passed on the way here to see if there are vacancies. Or we could make a move now.'

Without answering, Emma leans back in the passenger seat and watches through the window as a cargo ship inches its way across the horizon. She wonders who is on board and what they do to pass the time. Do they ever get seasick? Mesmerized by the gentle lapping of the waves, she has the urge to climb over the low barrier and throw herself into the water. It would put an end to all the heartbreak and pain, the tension and fear. If only they hadn't rescued her in the first place. Perhaps she would be with her father now instead of mourning him. Her mother might even be there too. And Rosa.

'Maybe we should go home now.' It is as though he is reading her thoughts.

Emma shakes her head. 'No, not yet. I want to see her, too.'

CHAPTER EIGHTEEN

The sun dips behind the darkened leaves. It is lower now, being pushed out of sight by autumn's arrival. She is still in the garden but standing by herself. Around her hordes of men and women are locked in their merry huddles. She scans the faces, searching for one that's familiar, but they are all strangers. Where is everyone? Her mother and father. Rosa. Dan. She cannot see them anywhere. Fear fills her mind at the thought of never seeing them again. But she needs to have hope. Maybe they are all together somewhere, perhaps in the house. But the house is no longer there. In its place stands a solitary oak tree, with branches laden with birds. Hundreds of tiny eyes stare back at her before flocking up into the darkness. The murmuration creates a shadow which she follows. It leads her to a building in the background where it disappears under the door. Relief runs through her because they must be inside waiting for her. As she approaches the rectangular stone hut a young woman runs out. It is Rosa, and she is grinning. Emma knows somebody else is inside but no longer wants to discover who that person is. Some things are best left concealed. The door opens.

***

The journey takes one hour exactly, and, apart from the robotic voice giving occasional directions, is silent. David drives at a leisurely pace insisting Emma just relaxes and enjoys the ride as if they were going somewhere out of this world. But rather than going to the moon and back, the destination is an isolated nursing home, a place that no one would choose to visit unless they wanted there. It will be the final stop in her trip down memory lane, and she knows it will be as painful as all the others. Despite the pain and heartache endured so far, it is still the only place she wants to be.

She's thought of little else since waking up in the hospital. Going home to her old world even if that world has passed on to the mysterious place where spent time goes. Because deep down she'd hoped it hadn't, and that somehow everything was just the way she'd left it the night she closed her eyes. The night she still can't remember. Yet maybe her mother hasn't gone completely. Maybe.

As they get closer to their destination, part of her wants David to drive even slower, to keep the hope alive for just a while longer. But the rational part of her mind knows the visit is long overdue, and there is no point in delaying the inevitable.

They pull into the carpark and sit quietly staring through the windscreen. Probably because he knows what's inside, David appears more nervous than Emma. Did he drive slowly in the hope that the doors would have closed to visitors by the time they got there? It is getting late, but relatives are visible through the many windows. They get out of the car and he opens the main door.

Emma walks through into a carpeted foyer and immediately the smell hits her - fresh flowers mixed with stale air. It takes her back to a moment in time, carrying a tray along a landing. She must have worked in a nursing home at some point, possibly while at university. How many millions of moments are now lost to her forever? And what if her condition is deteriorating rather than improving? How long before she herself is a resident in this very building?

'This way, Darling,' David says, already at the reception desk and holding out a pen.

Emma signs her name in the visitor's book below her husband's. *Emma Sims*. The first time she has used it herself. She scans the page on show. The dates only go back a few weeks, therefore, it is not so much of a surprise to see there are no other signatures next to the name Jennifer Watt. But it still breaks her heart to think of her mother sitting by herself week after week. At least she had the excuse of being in hospital. What about Susannah and ... whatever her son's name is? Couldn't they make the effort for their only surviving grandparent?

She can feel the anger building up inside her. But the anger is soon replaced by fear as she walks with David through a door into a grand dining room. Three uniformed women sit around the large wooden table in the centre. None of them notices the visitors intruding on their late dinner break. Finally, the nurse leading the way turns down a short corridor and stops outside a door at the end.

'She had a difficult night so is a bit sleepy this morning,' the nurse says as she opens the door. 'But I'm sure she'll be glad to see you.' Her words are directed at David rather than Emma whom she observes with curiosity. This is not lost on Emma as she steps past her into the room.

Jennifer Watt is sitting upright and watching a game show on television. At least that's how it first appears. As Emma and David approach, it is clear the elderly woman is not watching anything in the room. Her eyes are fixed, unreactive to any movement within their scope of vision. They are empty. They are lifeless.

Emma tries to swallow the grief that is rising up and about to overwhelm her. She fails miserably and rushes back out of the room, quickly followed by David. He holds her against his chest as she sobs uncontrollably. 'She doesn't know we're here.' She attempts to shake her closely held head. 'It's like she's dead.'

David kisses her head gently. 'No, Darling. She's tired, that's all. You heard what the nurse said. Your mother is catching up on her rest after a sleepless night.' Then he guides her back into the room. 'We've come this far. You can't leave without speaking to her,' he says gently.

Emma wants to scream out at him but manages to control her voice. 'But she won't even hear me.'

'We don't know that for certain. I've had interactions with her several times recently.'

I've had interactions with her. Not we. Emma lets this go for the moment as they approach Jennifer.

David sits in front of the lifeless woman confirming, as if there was any doubt, that she is unaware of her immediate surroundings, let alone her two visitors. With palpitations battering her chest, Emma sits down next to her mother. Her eyes fall on the older woman's left hand, withered and naked with no evidence of the delicate jewellery which once adorned it. Emma wonders where all her belongings are now. Have they been sold to pay for the care costs? How brutal the end of life is, she considers. Seventy years of material evidence of a person's existence swept away. Nothing remains of the younger Jennifer Watt. Her beauty, her class, her elegance. Nothing.

Emma takes the cold thin hand in her own and holds it to her cheek. 'I'm sorry I haven't been here for a while, Mum, but I was in hospital.' She kisses her mother's hand which is now wet with Emma's tears.

'Hello, Jennifer,' David says. 'Emma insisted on coming tonight even though she's still recovering.' His voice is patronising as if speaking to a child about another child. But it makes no difference. Jennifer doesn't flinch.

'How long has she been like this? Does she ever come around?' Emma's questions are aimed at the nurse, but she has already left the room. Seeing that David is now watching the television too, she settles back in her chair. At least she can share her mother's space for a short while. Still holding Jennifer's hand in hers, she closes her eyes and remembers a real moment from her past and every word spoken within it. Because there were only a few.

The doorbell sounds again. She has popped over unannounced, checking to see if they need any help with the last of the preparations. The mid-afternoon sun blasts its scorching rays onto her bare back as she stands at the unanswered door, and she begins to regret turning down Dan's offer to wait with her. Because of course, her parents would be in as where else would they be? The first guests would start arriving in a couple of hours. And Dan had to pick up their university friends from the train station and take them to the pub for an early drink. He will be okay to pick her up in an hour as he wouldn't dream of drinking in the daytime, especially if driving.

The door remains firmly closed, and she steps to the window and peers through several glass panes until able to make out something solid. Everything visible is inanimate – a bookcase, a desk, a piano. She crosses to the other front window and peers through again – a television, a settee, a coffee table. They must be at the back of the house. Or upstairs! After all, they weren't expecting anyone yet. Suddenly she wishes she could walk backwards out of the driveway and hide in the hedge until Dan comes back. Apprehensively she peers upwards towards the front bedroom window having to shield her eyes from the blasting sun to focus on the curtains. They hang motionless. Yet something is moving. A large red balloon floats above her, its long string hanging down beyond reach.

She walks around to the back garden and is met with a perfect arrangement of marquees and tables laid with unopened wine and upturned glasses. But still no parents.

They must have slipped out for something, she thinks, but then remembers the car in the driveway. The patio doors are unlocked, and she slips through them and into the kitchen diner. Two half-finished glasses of orange juice sit on the marble island in the centre of the room. Emma takes a sip from either glass. Both drinks are alcohol-free. And they are still cold so her parents must be here somewhere. Feeling uneasy, she decides to brave the upstairs rooms.

Calling out as she takes each step, Emma climbs to the top of the stairs where, at last, she hears quiet voices coming from her parents' bedroom.

'Mum! Dad!,' she shouts, loud enough for her voice to carry through the closed door. 'Is everything all right.'

There is no answer, so she taps on the panelled door before turning the handle. Suddenly her father's face meets hers. But it is not the face she knows so well. Rather it is filled with pained emotion. As if she were invisible, he brushes past without a word or other sign of acknowledgement. With a sinking feeling, she steps into the bedroom to another unfamiliar face. Her mother, sitting on the bed, is holding her stomach as if in severe pain. Emma rushes forwards and touches her cheeks.

'Mum, what's the matter? Should I phone for an ambulance?'

Her mother shakes her head and then stands ups. 'There's nothing wrong, Emma.' She moves to the dressing table and begins wiping the mascara stains from her upper cheeks. 'What are you doing here? You should be getting ready. The party starts in a couple of hours.'

Jennifer Watt begins the job of reapplying her makeup while her daughter stands watching her. The party might be going ahead, but any excitement has turned into a dark sense of foreboding.

'Darling.'

'Yes, Mum.' But this time the voice is male. 'Darling, she's awake.'

Emma takes a few seconds to readjust to the present situation. Her mother is still next to her but everything else is different. 'I'm sorry, David. Did you say something?'

'Yes, your mother is awake.'

For the first time, there is life in Jennifer's eyes. She turns her head and appears to focus on Emma's face for some time. Not wanting to spoil the moment, Emma holds her gaze and smiles.

'Hello, Mum. It's good to see you.' She kisses her mother's hand softly.

For a moment there is a confused expression on the older woman's face. Then her eyes narrow. She stiffens her hand and grasps Emma by the throat. For several seconds Emma is unable to react and can only watch the hatred in her mother's stare. It is hatred more intense than she has ever witnessed. Next there is a wall of blue blocking her view and she can breathe again. Blood-curdling cries fill the air.

Without knowing how she got there, Emma is standing outside the nursing home, her mother's cries still audible. David gently manoeuvres her into the car and starts the engine.

'I wonder what she saw when she looked at me.' Emma is talking to herself as much as to her companion.

'To be fair to her, she probably wasn't expecting to see two faces staring back at her when she woke from her daze.'

'She wasn't scared though, David. She was filled with hate. How could she hate me that much?'

'Don't be overdramatic, Darling. Whatever Jennifer was seeing back there, it wasn't you. Her mind is not what it was.'

'Of course, I know that but ...' She rubs her neck still feeling the sting of her mother's fingernails. 'I suppose we should go inside.'

They've been sitting in the car for ten minutes with the engine turned off, and the air around them is turning cold. And Emma is tired of feeling cold.

As they approach the front entrance a soft light switches on, illuminating them like some glitzy Hollywood couple. She steps back as he opens the door before he returns the favour, allowing her to enter first. The hallway is a mixture of dim light and shadows, and she observes how little it seems like a hotel, a place for travellers to settle in for the night. It feels more like they are sneaking into someone else's house. But then he closes the door and a hall light activated by movement switches on. This adds a soft glow to the large space. David touches her shoulder gently and whispers:

'Wait here and I'll check in.'

Once again Emma is alone with only her thoughts for company. She tries to take an interest in the oil paintings of strangers dotted around the dark-painted walls. But it doesn't hold back the avalanche of emotions that, within seconds, are sweeping over her. Intense grief, confusion, doubt, fear. The last is the most immediate one to face.

It would have been easier to go "home" knowing there would be separate bedrooms waiting for them. But despite the terrible experiences at the old house and nursing home, Emma has insisted on delaying the return journey. The country roads dominating much of the route home would have been particularly hazardous in the dimming light, and she knows David is tired. Why should he have to battle his way through winding roads at such a late hour merely because his wife is scared of spending the night with him?

And she is scared ... terrified. There is little point in convincing herself that she is the same age as David. It never works. But she reminds herself that a woman of twenty-three is still a woman. A grown-up. And there are plenty of young women who marry older men. Particularly successful men.

'We have a carpark view.' David has reappeared and is holding up a room key. 'Do you want to freshen up before dinner?'

We. Emma smiles, forcing back down the wail of protest rising up in her throat. There is no last-minute reprieve. The moment has arrived.

Like Emma, the room is tired and in need of a good polish and there is a slight musty odour which is comforting rather than unpleasant. With dark wood furniture and the floor covered with a thin-pile cream and sage carpet, it reminds Emma of her grand-parents' front room. Or does she need to find something homely and comforting to distract herself?

Trying to avoid looking at the small double bed, she walks over to the window, pulls up the sash and breathes in the night

air. Directly below their window is David's car and she wonders if he arranged this. He seems the cautious type who would do everything necessary to protect his property. A shiver runs through her at the thought of being part of that property. And at this very moment, she can sense him standing close behind her.

'I've run you a bath.'

Turning around, she keeps her head down to avoid meeting his face in such close proximity. 'Thanks. That's just what I need,' she says, before rushing into the sanctuary of the ensuite bathroom.

CHAPTER NINETEEN

Emma is leaning against the wall and gripping a bottle of lager. The room has a strange odour which is making her feel dizzy and sick. She shouldn't have had so much to drink. Rosa is there in a cobalt blue dress that could have been made to match her eyes. As she spins around, the full-length mirror reflects her every angle as if she were everywhere in the room, darting around like a kingfisher in flight. The young men pretend not to see her in case their girlfriends are watching them watching her. Because they are watching, too. Just like Emma. Even Rosa watches herself as she dances and laughs and drinks. She senses someone staring at her from somewhere in the room, but she cannot see his face. Or her face. But she knows it isn't Dan because he is looking for her outside. Her arm begins to sting, and she is certain Rosa is squeezing it. But when she turns her head there is no one there. She looks back and everyone else has disappeared. She stands alone in the room which is becoming darker by the second. Then a man's face appears in the gloom. Too fuzzy to identify, he runs forward and pushes her against the wall. The bottle falls to the floor. She tries to scream but his mouth is on hers. With all her might, she pushes him back and he falls onto the broken glass. Now he is covered in blood.

***

In one corner of an otherwise empty hotel lounge, Emma and David are sitting on separate chairs, watching flames dancing in the hearth. Piped music adds to the relaxing atmosphere and, if it weren't for the rawness of the day's trauma, Emma could imagine she was on a date. Would it be the first, second or third? She takes another gulp of wine rather than eat any more of the pizza resting on her lap. They were too late for a proper evening meal but she's not that hungry. Besides, her dreams are crazy enough without eating cheese so late. David appears to share her view as he's barely touched his plate either.

Clean and warm at last, Emma could happily close her eyes for the next eight hours, even while sitting upright. When was the last time she had that sort of mental rest? It certainly wasn't while in the hospital, so it must be months, at least. Possibly the night before the party. But not the party she's been dreaming about. Because that was decades ago.

'Shall I order another Malbec?' David asks.

She glances at the empty bottle on the table and then back at her near-drained glass. Has she really drunk that much? I shouldn't have anymore, she wants to say, but that would bring the next stage of the night closer. And she doesn't want to start that part yet.

'Okay. But don't let me drink much more,' she replies.

He walks to the bar, and Emma strains to hear the music trickling from the sole speaker on the far wall. Each tune sounds vaguely familiar but not quite enough to identify. She decides it must be one of those big band albums her mother loved but her father hated. *Monstrosities*, he would call them. *The vandalism of perfection*. But Emma likes them, too. There is something about the jaunty beat and blasts of brass that raise her spirits. Yes, she isn't so unlike her mum. How she misses her.

'You're thinking of Jennifer, aren't you?' David says as he pours more wine into Emma's glass. 'Don't worry. We'll visit her again, soon. I'm sure she'll recognise you next time.'

Emma smiles. 'I was remembering her in happier times. But those times are over, so I'll have to get used to her in the present.' She takes another sip of wine.

'You need to do both, Darling. We don't have to leave the past behind us. It can remain alive in our memories.'

Alive in our memories. Or her dreams? They are all so vivid, so real. Especially Rosa.

'Emma watch!'

She jumps at the urgency in David's voice before steadying herself just in time to straighten her glass. 'Sorry. We shouldn't really be drinking red wine in this room,' she says, looking at the luxurious cream carpet beneath her feet. Putting down her glass, she picks up a slice of pizza and nibbles at it. 'David, do you ever dream?'

He tilts his head in surprise at the question. 'I don't know.

Probably. Doesn't everyone dream?'

'That's a rather strange answer,' she says. 'You should know if you dream.'

Shrugging his shoulders, he replies, 'Not necessarily. Dreams belong in the great black void our minds dip into during sleep.'

'Do you think the great black void is Death?'

He wipes spilt wine from his chin. 'Good grief, woman, where did that come from?'

'Well, nobody really knows, do they?'

'Wherever our dreams take place, they remain there. They don't follow us back into wakefulness. So, no, in answer to your original question, I don't know whether I dream, or not.' He gulps the remainder of the wine in his glass. 'What's brought you onto this bizarre topic?'

Dutch courage has doused Emma's nerves. Her mind is now filled with daring words and her tongue loosened. Suddenly, she feels as though David is her closest confidant. 'Because lately, I have dreamt every night, and even during the day. And the dreams are so real, David, like they are not dreams at all but vivid memories. I can almost feel the people, hear their voices, smell their scent.'

His eyes flash with irritation, or is it hurt before he asks, 'And who are the people in your dreams, Emma?'

'My parents … and you. But mostly of Rosa. I know this is going to sound crazy, but I think she is trying to speak to me, David.'

He laughs at her. 'Really! And what sort of things does she say, Darling?'

Emma shakes her head. 'Okay, she doesn't speak to me. But I think she is showing something to me, but it's all too muddled to make sense of.'

'Well, give me an example. What does she show you?'

'My life ... in order. It's like having it flashed before my eyes but in the wrong direction. It started with school and now it's reached the last place I can ...'

'You can what?' 'I can remember.'

'And where was that?'

She takes a deep breath. 'My parents' party. The night of my first accident ... of Rosa's death. And she's always there in my dreams. I think she's going to show me how she died, and ...'

'And what?'

'And who killed her.'

She waits for him to respond, but he remains silent. Either he is speechless, or too drunk to say anymore. The second bottle of wine sits empty on the table. Or is it the third? She cannot remember. They sit together in total silence, the piped music now switched off. Even the fire has died out. In the background, she notices the barman wiping the counter and removing beermats. It is time to retire for the night.

David stands up, knocking the table as he does so. 'Are you ready to go up?'

She nods.

As soon as she steps into the room, he pulls her tight into his arms and kisses her passionately. It takes her by surprise and she finds herself unable to react. Instead, she stands frozen while he removes his clothes before turning his attention back to her. As he unbuttons her blouse, she fixes her eyes on his naked torso. Her heart pounds to the point of pain but she knows it's not through desire. Yet she tells herself that it will all be over soon, and she can fall back into the other world, the great black void. Just get through it. Now she is naked, too, and he is lying on top of her, their bodies pressed tight. She closes her eyes but that cannot shut out the panic within her. It is no good.

'Stop! Get off me!'

He moves away, saying, 'It's okay. Don't worry.'

'I'm sorry, but I can't,' she cries, before grabbing some clothing and running into the bathroom.

Her violent retches are drowned out by the uneven clattering of the ventilator above the bath. It is a hellish noise, though not loud enough to shut out David's pleading voice. He is apologetic. He says he rushed her. He offers to sleep on the floor. Crouched on the bathmat, wrapped in a towel, she ignores him. The air from the ventilator blows cold on her bare shoulders, but she closes her eyes and imagines she's outside lying under the night sky. Or on a boat. Yes, a boat would be more real.

Seawater laps over the sides as they push against the waves. Her clothes and hair are soaked, her body frozen. She is out of the water, no longer drowning, but can feel nothing. She must be dead. There is somebody else on the boat because it is moving forward. Wooden blades flash against the dark sky, oars struggling against gravity. A woman is rowing the boat, but she is too small and weak to bash through the waves. They are no longer moving forward but being thrown into the air before crashing down on the foamy seawater. Now the boat is listing and tilting, and the oars are drifting away from them. The woman is in the water, her dark hair sprawled out like seaweed. She is facedown and will soon be dead like her. Somehow they float closer to each other until their sodden bodies touch. Touch? If she can feel, she must still be alive. She grabs the woman's hair, lifting her head from the water. No. It can't be. This makes no sense.

She jumps up from the bathmat, her body aching from lying on the near-hard surface. Above her, the ventilator is still clattering but there is only silence beyond the bathroom door. She splashes her face with water in an attempt to clear the mist from her mind. But water cannot wash away the utter confusion, the madness, the insanity. She thought she could deal with losing her mind, but she was wrong. This is worse than any physical illness.

David is asleep. His snores are light but his sleep is heavy, fuelled by the evening's wine. Having turned the bathroom light off, Emma attempts to feel around for her scattered clothes. An electric pain pierces the sole of her foot as she steps on something cold and sharp, causing her to curse out loud. She holds her breath. The dark mass on the bed remains still. Deciding it is worth the risk, she shuffles over to the bed with her arm outstretched until it touches the bedside lamp. The glow is soft but sufficient. One garment at a time, Emma picks up the clothes she has worn since leaving the hospital before returning to the bathroom.

She is ready to leave. Picking up the bunch of keys that caused her so much pain, she takes a last look at David. He is lying on his back, but his eyes are closed and he is sleeping soundly. Without warning, guilt bashes her conscience. He doesn't deserve this again. But she needs to see this through and, if he knew where she was going, he would stop her.

She lifts the blankets from one side of the bed to cover his naked body. It is one wifely thing she can do at least. As she is pulling the sheet above his waist, he sighs and his body shifts. Frozen to the spot, Emma can only watch as David turns over onto his side. She watches his back for a sign that he is waking up. One, two, three. No movement. It is okay. She can go.

But something is stopping her, something she can see on his back. Three scars, small but ugly. An image flashes through her mind for the second time – an angry man pushing her against the wall before falling onto a broken bottle. It was David in that dream. But why was he trying to hurt her? What had she done to anger him so? It must have been something to do with Dan. A stab of guilt hits her not for the first time. To think she married a man who'd behaved so violently towards her. It's insane!

The hotel door is a slight barrier but, after searching behind the reception for the key, Emma steps into the fresh early morning air.

Within seconds, she is inside David's car with the engine running. Did she ever pass her driving test? It doesn't matter. She presses a button, types in the name of her destination and then puts the car into first gear.

The dawn air bites at her naked arms as she walks along the canal path. The stagnant water seems to be taunting her with its silence. Not a ripple spoils the stillness. Even the impact of her shoes on the gravel beneath is cushioned by the littering of fallen leaves. She feels as though she's in a state of limbo, striding forward in search of the way out. Perhaps she is, but right now the exit is not her target.

It must be somewhere along here, she thinks. She hopes. To her joy, David's top-of-the-range car had a visual map on the dashboard allowing her to retrace her steps. Using the first train stop as a starting point, she'd estimated the area of the canal on which he could be. Two and a half miles per hour, that's all a barge can do. Then there are the locks and rest stops. Dan couldn't have gone far. She peers into the distance but there is no dark bulk parked up. Perhaps he's made slower progress than she thought and she's started too far along. Her heart sinks at the thought of walking back the same distance and more. Just as she thinks it's hopeless, the moon appears in the sky shining a silvery beam through the darkness. There he is.

Once again, she dares to intrude into his private world, the world she drove him to. How will he react this time? Each step brings her closer to finding out. He will be irritated by her sense of entitlement; she is certain of that. How dare she come along bringing with her the hurt and regret of a time long gone? Just because her life is now terrible as well.

The tiny shape in the distance has increased to its actual size. Her feet are rooted to the floor waiting for instructions, but Emma does not know the way forward. A three-foot gap stands between her and the edge of the barge, too far for her to attempt to jump. If only she were younger.

She stares at the canvas door willing it to open. At least that would save her from performing the outrage of opening it herself. Something darker than the sky touches her head. Black wings catch in her hair, and she screams. Emma watches the bat as it flies up the length of the canal until it vanishes. When she readjusts her eyes, they are met by a figure standing on the bow.

'Why are you here, again?' Dan asks. His voice is dispassionate rather than cold.

Emma gasps. In the dim light, he looks the same as when he was twenty-five, when he was her fiancé, when he still loved her. She walks towards him.

'Stop!'

The frantic command shakes Emma out of her trance-like state. Peering down she realises how close she is to the edge of the path. A few inches more and she'd have fallen through the gap and into the murky depths below. Without stepping back, she looks at Dan. The few feet of water between them might just as well be an ocean. Yet somehow, she knows he still loves her. 'I know the truth now,' she says, without moving her eyes.

He shrugs. 'What truth?'

'The truth about Rosa. You were right. She was jealous and destructive, tearing other people's lives apart because she couldn't bear them to be happier than her.'

He gives a scornful response. 'So, you've come all the way out here to tell me what I told you yesterday. Perhaps there really is a problem with your memory.'

'But I do remember now. I wasn't angry at Rosa because I thought she was seeing you behind my back; it was because she was seeing Dad.'

Dan doesn't flinch. His silence is as good as an acknowledgement. Behind him the sky has turned pink, softening his rigid pose.

Emma continues. 'That's who the condoms belonged to, wasn't it? The ones I found hidden in our wardrobe.'

'You should have said you'd found them,' Dan says quietly. 'Then I would have told you.'

'So, you covered up for Dad, saying he was with you when they were together in some seedy hotel.'

He shakes his head. 'I thought it would fizzle out, that she would get bored and go back to London or America. It was just a silly midlife fling. But if you or Jennifer found out, things could never go back to the way they were.'

'Did my mother find out?'

'Kind of. She sensed he was being unfaithful but didn't know who with. That's why she hired a private detective.'

'And that private detective was David, wasn't it?'

He nods. 'Sims was skint when he began working for the firm, so he took on a bit of moonlighting.'

'Did you know he was working for my mother?'

'No. When we moved to the London office, I saw her hanging around. I had no idea she was meeting him.'

'She must have been angry with you, too.' Emma laughs to herself. 'For a while, I wondered if the two of you were having an affair.'

'She came to the office to ask me straight out.'

'And you confirmed her suspicions.'

'There was no point in denying them because she already knew. She said she could smell her on him. It made me sick when she told me that.'

'But she didn't want to lose Dad, did she? That's why she changed her appearance. She wanted to look young like Rosa.'

'Your mother was full of class, not the trash that ghastly woman was. She was torn apart by the betrayal.'

Torn apart. 'I suppose that's why my mother and I fell out. She must have blamed me for bringing Rosa into our home. And she was right.'

'What are you talking about? You and Jennifer never fell out.'

'Yes, we did. David said we fell out years ago.'

'Huh! And you believed him? You and your mother may not always have seen eye to eye, especially over ... us, but you were close enough.'

Emma struggles to absorb Dan's words. She desperately wants to believe what he is saying because it would lessen the pain a little.

The thought of being estranged from her mother for so many valuable years is torturous. And did David actually say that or was it just a misinterpretation of his words on her part? But her voice breaks as she recalls her visit to the nursing home. 'My mother attacked me, Dan. She hated me.'

'She's got dementia!' There's the hint of a grin on his face, but the tone is playful rather than scorning.

Dementia. Is that what she's going through too? 'How would you know this, Dan? You are stuck out here in your own off-grid world so how would you know anything about me and my mother?'

'Because Jon and I were always in touch. We were friends, remember.'

A feeling of contentment rises up through Emma's body as she visualises her father and Dan continuing their relationship. She wonders if they played golf again though doesn't waste time asking. For the moment she is filled with love for the man standing a few feet away. He has provided her with some peace of mind regarding her family post-Rosa. Rosa. There is only one more question to ask. 'Dan, did David kill Rosa?'

Not even a second passes before Dan scoffs. 'Huh! Do you think I would keep that secret? Whatever put that idea into your head?'

'I saw his ... his back.' The words make her feel as if she were the unfaithful one. 'There were scars, and I remember he fell onto that bottle ... at the party. He must have been very angry after that.'

Although Dan's features are still obscured by the dimness of the dawn light, Emma knows his face is screwed up in confusion. This is confirmed when he speaks.

'So, he got into a scuffle with you and Rosa, got drunk then fell on broken glass. Your neighbour drove him straight to casualty to get stitched up but they admitted him. He knew it was his own fault, no one else's so I can't see why he'd want to kill her even if it had been possible.'

Now Emma is thrown into utter confusion. She was so certain about David. Or was it just wishful thinking? It would have been a convenient way out of the marriage.

'Is that all?' Dan's voice is harsh but weak.

His slight tremble is not lost on Emma who senses he is nervous. And there must be a reason why.

'So, if David didn't kill Rosa, it was someone else. And you know who that was, don't you?'

A deafening silence descends in the space between them. His eyes have drifted upwards as if he is looking to the changing sky for inspiration. His thoughts are guarded, but he knows the answer to her question. That much is clear. She waits patiently for him to focus on her once more, but he seems in a trance.

She inches forward to try to break into his thoughts. 'Dan, why won't you answer me? Is the truth so terrible?' She exhales before daring to vocalise what is now bashing around inside her head. 'Dan, did my father kill her?'

The sound of her own words is like a dagger to her heart. No sooner have they left her lips than she wants to drag them back inside her numb brain. But it is too late. She can see Dan's chest rising and falling against the creeping flame of sunrise behind him. Finally, his eyes meet hers and he speaks again.

'Your father was a fool. He was willing to crush his family over that slut. I'm convinced that contributed to Jennifer's illness. She couldn't deal with the reality of no longer being young enough for her husband. And it was all for nothing. It pains me to say it, but he deserved to live with that guilt for the rest of his life. And live with it he did. We need to let it die with him too.'

'No, you have to tell me. Did he kill Rosa?' Water is seeping through her shoes as she moves closer to the edge.

'Emma, stand back. You're going to fall in.'

'I don't care. Why won't you answer me?'

'Because you already know. Just open your eyes and you'll have all the answers.' He is shouting, his voice sounding like a ship horn bellowing. It no longer sounds human.

For a moment, she is in a trance-like state hypnotised by the healing glow of the distant sunrise. She wishes it were nearer, that she could reach out her hand and touch the magical rays, go through the blazing dawn glory into a world far away. A better world. Her body is swaying, and she can feel herself falling forward but she keeps her eyes on the horizon. The ship horn is blaring out now. She is floating, her feet no longer on the ground. Something touches her head. A hand. Now she is falling down, sinking into the cold, wet darkness.

She's falling into nothingness, hurtling downwards through a vacuum. It feels as though she is tumbling forward and backwards simultaneously. There is no logic or reason. Nothing is rational in this unknown space. Out of this world, or inside her own mind? There is no time, no sound, no life. So much darkness but there are no shadows. It is too dark for shadows. Where are the stars and the moon? She is desperate to see the light once more.

Chapter Twenty

She watches them in the garage. It is the only place they can be alone. Jon kisses her passionately, his eyes burning with more than desire. With love. *Meet me on the cliff path in ten minutes. I have a surprise for you, my Rosamunde.* She is his Rosamunde, and he loves to serenade her. Rosa sings the melody as she runs back to the party to collect her coat. But Emma, her eyes filled with hate, starts shouting at her. And David, too. Now everyone is looking at them. So, she leaves them all behind, running until she finds him again. She is leaving everything behind her as she runs up the cliff path: her friend, her family, her life. Nothing will be as it was. For the first time, she will feel what it's like to love and be loved. There he is, standing tall and proud. He is holding something in his hand ... a box. Smiling at her, he lifts the lid and the inside sparkles like Venus. She is crying with happiness because they will be together at last. But she cannot take the ring because her arm is bleeding. Jennifer is crying too. Why is she here? Jon is shouting, trying to stop her. But there is no escape from the knife.

***

When she opens her eyes, she can see her reflection staring back. No, it is not her face. It is Susanna's. She is sitting to the right of the bed. Now she is speaking.

'You've come back. I can't tell you how relieved we all are.' Her voice sounds different. Despite the words spoken, the tone is cold and distant.

'Where's your father?'

Her face crumples. 'He's at the police station. Dan's there too doing whatever he can to help.'

'Dan? Is he going to represent him?'

'Not Dad, no. He's going to represent Mum.'

'Mum? But I'm ...'

'She's been arrested for attempted murder. It is a less serious charge though Dan says attempted murder will be easier to prove. Obviously, the prosecution will have you as their star witness.'

'Susanna, you're making no sense.'

'Who's Susanna?'

Thelma enters the room and smiles warmly. Why is she wearing a nurse's uniform? 'Hello, Dear. It's good to see you awake. Let's take a listen to your pulse.' She lifts the still limp arm and counts the faint beats. 'Sounding good. The doctor will be in shortly,' she says, as she departs.

'I thought Thelma was a teacher, not a nurse.'

'Who's Thelma?'

'My friend. My only friend.'

'You mean Emma not Thelma. And I'm not a nurse or a teacher. And as for friends like you, who needs enemies?'

She refocuses her stinging eyes on the visitor. Once again, it is like looking in a mirror, a magical mirror because it is a younger version of herself. But it is not Susanna. And it is not her. She turns her head to the side searching for a way out of the fog. There it is. 'Please, pass me the mirror.'

The face is smooth with skin unblemished, the hair natural with its soft red curls visible through the grit, and azure eyes still glistening with youth. Red curls. Azure eyes. 'I'm Rosa, and I'm alive.'

Emma nods. 'Yes, you are. And we are all glad you made it back. At least it won't be a murder charge.'

How many minutes have passed since she woke up? Ten? Sixty? She's not even certain she is awake. Rosa's confusion is pushed to the back of her mind as she absorbs the caustic atmosphere between her and the young woman still sitting by the bed. 'You really hate me, don't you?'

'Of course, I hate you. You tried to rip my family apart and destroyed the relationship with the man I loved.'

'But what happened with you and Dan? He had nothing to do with ... us.'

'Us! Don't you dare use that word. My father never wants to see you again, do you hear? He says it was just a silly midlife crisis and you took advantage of him when he was at his most depressed. And

Dan covered up for the squalid affair. How could I ever trust him again?'

Yet it sounds like you've forgiven Jon, Rosa wants to say. 'What about Jennifer?'

'Well, as my mother will be going to prison for a long time, it hardly matters how she feels. But Dad is standing by her. It's the least he can do.'

Rosa agrees that it probably for the best. However she felt about Jon in the past, those feelings have yet to come back to her. Hopefully, they never will. 'You must hate me so much, Emma. I wonder why you're even here.'

Emma laughs bitterly before standing up and leaning over Rosa. 'Do you know how difficult it was for me to sit here willing you to pull through when all I really wanted to do was put a pillow over your face until you stopped breathing for-'

'Uh... can I come in?'

Both women look up at the young man standing in the doorway. Wearing a tracksuit bottom and a loose t-shirt, he could be a visitor if it wasn't for the slippers on his feet.

'What do you want, David?' Emma snaps.

'To prevent things getting out of hand for a second time,' he says, stepping inside the room. 'Come on, Emma. Why don't you go home? There's no point in staying here, now.'

Emma opens her mouth but the expected tirade remains inside. Instead, she glares at Rosa before pushing past a wincing David who steps into the vacated space.

'I'm sure she didn't mean that. She's under a lot of stress.' Rosa stares at the man now standing at her bedside; tall, lean, and good-looking despite the grimacing expression he is trying to keep hidden. For months, he was the co-star in the fictitious world inside her head, playing the role of a stranger but becoming her husband and protector. But none of that was real. Now, in reality, he is merely a bit part player, a colleague of a boyfriend of a friend. Once again, a virtual stranger.

'Do you want me to go, Rosa? I don't want to cause you any more upset.'

He sounds so caring. 'It's okay … David. But what are you doing here? Why are you a patient, too?'

He lifts his t-shirt to reveal his heavily wrapped torso. 'A piece of glass pierced a kidney … just. I guess it'll teach me to mind my own business.'

Images of David's scarred back flash through her mind. Was it really just a dream? 'I pushed you over at the party, didn't I? That's why you fell on the glass.'

'Hey! It wasn't your fault. I shouldn't have taken the job in the first place. Jennifer was better off not knowing about the affair.'

The affair. The dispassionate way David speaks makes the situation even more bizarre. Part of Rosa wants to ask him about his own dreams as a patient. Did he dream about her? 'So, Jennifer hired you to find out if Jon was being unfaithful. How did you find out?'

'I followed you to the house. There was no other reason for you to be there.'

'But we could have denied it. Why was it enough to convince Jennifer?'

For the first time, David's face displays confusion. 'Rosa, you were there. Jon decided it was the right time to tell Jennifer, and you were over the moon about it. It was then I realised that I'd made things much worse. If I hadn't confronted you both, the affair may well have fizzled out. Instead, I brought everything to a head. At the party, Jon told Jennifer and she went crazy.'

'But why did I push you onto the glass?'

'You don't remember that, do you? I was trying to stop you meeting him. I begged you to finish things but you laughed at me. That's when I pushed you into the wall. I was trying to stop you leaving but my actions were disgraceful.'

So were mine, Rosa thinks. 'What will happen to Jennifer?'

He shakes his head. 'That depends on the charge. Obviously, she's not saying anything, at the moment.' 'Obviously?'

'Yes. Dan's advising her. They'll have to make some sort of statement now you've regained consciousness. Jon's already told the police he was with Jennifer at the time of the incident. That's a huge mistake, in my opinion. He could end up in prison himself.'

'Jon ... in prison.'

'Yes. It's clearly a false alibi. I don't know what he was thinking of. Guilt, I suppose. But that won't work now you're able to give your account. I expect she'll claim it was an accident, that she never meant for you to fall off the cliff. That won't explain the cuts on your arm, however.'

Rosa notices her one arm is heavily bandaged. Pressing the fabric until able to feel the pain, she realises how very lucky she is to be alive. The pain will disappear then she can start her life afresh. But what about everyone else? 'David, I can explain the cuts. And it's not what you think.'

Thelma is back in the room, her face glowing with kindness. 'Hello, Darling. The porters will be here soon to take you down to day surgery. We're going to patch up that arm for you so it's as good as new. I hope that other patient hasn't been hanging around again. You need to rest.'

'I feel like I've been resting for months,' Rosa says. 'It's not as though visitors are queuing up at the door. David's the only person who seems to care.'

'Hey, now, that young woman has barely left your side. She's been sitting there with her notebook, recording every single movement then grilling us about the significance of each blink and breath. Whatever she said, she cares about you.'

The nurse's words are as soothing as any ointment and Rosa wants to hug her. 'Thanks, Thelma.'

'And then, there was that other young man.'

'Who was that?'

'The policeman. Yes, he was here a couple of times, too.'

Rosa's heart jumps. How could he have followed her into this world? 'Was it Detective Carr?'

'Hahaha. He wasn't really a policeman. Only, some actor friend trying to wheedle his way past the on-duty staff. But your friend, David, knew straight away and told him to leave.'

Actor friend. Joe? So he's come all this way even after she turned him down. He really must care about her. 'Is he here now?'

'Not now. Only those other detectives, the real ones.'

'Oh, yes. I need to speak to them, too. Can you get them for me?'

'No, I can't. They've been sitting around here for three days. Another day won't hurt.'

Three days. Is that all it's been? She looks around the room as though it could give her the answer. Next to the bed, a cabinet is covered with gifts – fruit, flowers, chocolates, and a china doll. 'Could you pass me that doll, please?'

The nurse picks up the doll and passes it to Rosa. 'Here you are. Don't drop it. Matron took some persuading to allow this in here because it would smash into tiny pieces if someone knocked it over. But, due to your mother not being able to visit herself ...'

'So, she sent this instead.' Rosa stares at her favourite old toy, its black shiny hair, white face and red lips. 'I called her Snow White because I loved Disney princesses.'

'Every girl is a princess, Sweetheart.'

Rosa smiles. 'Yes, I know that now.' She hands the doll back to the nurse. 'Please could I speak to those detectives before I go down to surgery?'

Shaking her head the nurse says, 'Let's wait a while.'

'Please, Thelma. It'll only take a few minutes.'

She puts her hands on her wide hips before wagging one finger at Rosa. 'All right, a few minutes. And it's Tina, not Thelma.

***

Six weeks later

An array of golden leaves blows like confetti, giving the watery path a magical sheen, like the Yellow Brick Road. Rosa pulls the zip of his jacket up to her chin to protect herself against the early morning air. But to feel the crisp breeze against her cheeks is invigorating, and for the first time since leaving hospital, she feels fully alive.

'We'll need to stop for some sugar in the next village,' he says, as he hands her a mug.

'Or you could give up sugar in your tea, Joe,' she replies, combing his tousled light blond hair with her free hand. 'A life on the ocean waves calls for some personal sacrifices.

'Ha! Listen to the woman who refuses to drink out of a cup with a microscopic chip in.'

Touché!, she thinks but does not say. There's nothing wrong with having a few airs and graces for a change, even with a man who loves you for the person you really are. Joe had been there in the hospital, talking to her, trying to pull her out of the coma. As well as gorgeous, he is kind and caring and, since waking up, she has looked at him through different eyes.

November wasn't an ideal time to begin a six-month trip around the waterways of England, but Rosa felt like the challenge of surviving a winter on water. Besides, she had nowhere else to go having given up both her rented bedsit and the old beach house. And how could she show her face in Pickford so soon after what happened? No, it's best to let the Watt family glue their lives back together ... if that is in any way possible. To give it the best chance, Rosa needs to be as far away as possible.

Nobody was surprised when the attempted murder charge was dropped. Once Rosa "confessed" to the police about her "botched suicide attempt", the case was closed. Although the police suspected Rosa was lying, there was little they could do. Even the false alibi charge was a no-go. Rosa claimed to have seen Mr and Mrs Watt going into their bedroom as she smuggled a knife out of the kitchen. When asked why she'd bothered taking the knife with her, Rosa said she didn't want to drown like Ophelia.

'One of your many acting roles, I take it.' one detective had replied.

In contrast to the detectives, Joe doesn't want to know the minute details of Rosa's *dice with death,* being only too glad it failed. He is, however, baffled as to why they'd suspected Jennifer Watt of attempted murder in the first place. Nor is Rosa willing to shed any light on this mystery.

A middle-aged couple walking their dog on the canal path wave as the barge sails past. Instinctively, Joe wraps his arm around Rosa's waist. 'We'll pull over at the first sight of a phone box,' he says, before kissing the top of her head.

Rosa nods. 'Yes, he said it wouldn't be long.'

'To be honest, I'm surprised he offered to take up your mother's appeal case after you put him in hospital.'

Giving Joe a playful dig with her elbow, Rosa says, 'Hey! He didn't blame me for that. He always says it wasn't my fault.'

'Whatever you say.' Joe's attention has moved to the lock which is now visible. 'We've got heavy work ahead. Are you ready?

But Rosa is looking behind the barge, her thoughts not yet moved away from the last conversation.

'Yes, David Sims is a good man. I don't know what I'd do without him.'

OTHER BOOKS BY MARIE SIBBONS

ForgetMeNot

P rologue

The narrow stairs creaked at every third step taken as if they were telling her to turn around. Although alone in the house, she winced at each sound she made as she climbed towards the attic room. White silvery clouds were lending a shimmering glow to the otherwise dark room. Her reflection appeared in the cracked windowpane as she took the final step onto the ragged carpet. Taking off her glasses as she moved closer to the image, she could see the blotches under both eyes. They reminded her of the disappointment she had experienced a few hours earlier. And yet the day had started so hopefully. Maybe it wasn't over yet. No. It is over and she must accept it.

Crouching to open the tiny cupboard door, she looked down to see a teardrop splashing onto the wooden box that she was holding. She recalled her conversation with that old woman in the nursing home which had made her feel so ashamed. It was time to move on with her own life and not dwell on someone else's past. Tomorrow would be a new day, different from all the others. She placed the box inside the cupboard and closed the door for the last time.

Then she heard the stairs creak.

ONEDEADLYSECRET

Lara's eyes fixed on the dark wooden door in front of her. Behind it was the answer to a question, the question that had dominated her life for so long. After twenty years of extreme emotions, she had no idea how she would feel when the door finally opened. When it did, her emotions remained buried deep inside.

He was just as she expected him to be. He did not turn his scrawny face to look at her when she walked into the small room where he and several suited men and women were sitting. How could she tell if he was truly remorseful when she couldn't see into his eyes, the windows of his soul? As if reading her mind, he lifted his head and turned his cold, beady blue eyes to meet hers. There was no remorse; she could tell that immediately. Yet he had convinced the parole board to the contrary.

The man dressed in the least expensive suit, who had guided Lara into the room, sat down next to her. With his softly softly approach he'd persuaded Lara to contribute to the deluge of information that the Hugo Boss suits had to consider. Those men and women would need to decide the extent of the risk the convict posed to the community he would be going back to after twenty years. What had prison life been like for him? Twenty years was a long time to be well-behaved. And did he now regret the heinous crime he had committed all those years ago?

Her hands were shaking as she unfolded the statement that she was dreading reading out. It was brief, like the time she'd had with her sister. All she could say was that she missed Bella and grieved for the future relationship that they'd both been robbed of. It didn't matter to the panel. That she could also tell. They feigned sympathy but they had already made their decision. Tom Bailey would be released.

Outside the courtroom, Lara thanked the victim liaison officer and hurried back to her car. Bailey would be back on the streets within weeks, but at least he wouldn't be anywhere near her. That was the first and last time she would have to see him.

Then the realisation slammed into her like a steel bar - she had seen him before, those cruel blue eyes, that smirk, the tiny scar on his left cheek. Suddenly, it was clear - he didn't feel remorse because there was nothing to feel remorse for. He didn't kill Bella. Someone else did.

Printed in Great Britain
by Amazon